Alicia Cook

T0210217

caitlyn siehl

COURTNEY
PEPPERNELL

K.Y.
ROBINSON

TYLER
KNOTT
GREGSON

WILDER

KOMAL
KAPOOR

[DIS]CONNECTED

POEMS & STORIES OF

CONNECTION AND

OTHERWISE

EDITED BY MICHELLE HALKET

VOLUME TWO

RAQUEL
FRANCO

NOAH
MILLIGAN

N.L.
SHOMPOLE

ALICIA
COOK

CAITLYN
SIEHL

central
avenue
publishing

2019

Published by Central Avenue Publishing, an imprint of Central Avenue
Marketing Ltd.
www.centralavenuepublishing.com

**[Dis]Connected: Poems & Stories of Connection and Otherwise
Volume 2**

978-1-77168-180-3 (pbk)
978-1-77168-181-0 (epub)
978-1-77168-182-7 (mobi)

Published in Canada

Printed in United States of America

1. FICTION / Short Stories - Multiple Authors   2. POETRY / General

10 9 8 7 6 5 4 3 2 1

For the poets and writers and artists.

Introduction

Sometime in 2017, someone told me they heard poetry was the next adult colouring book, referring to the craze of the early/mid-2010s. They made it sound like it was a fad that would soon die out.

That opinion made me so mad that I decided to prove them wrong and show them that there's more to contemporary poets than the short snippets we see on social media. I decided to publish an anthology of poetry and short fiction. So many found the idea so interesting (there were articles and reviews and a whirlwind of activity at trade shows), that I decided to do it again.

In the first edition, I invited the poets I liked and asked them to recommend other, as-yet-unknown poets who were just getting started. As a result of that exercise, and because those poets are just plain hardworking and talented individuals, many of them went on to publish their own collections.

Working on the first edition proved to entail a lot of sweat and tears—definitely on my part. But it was a labour of love and at the end of the process I held this beautiful book in my hand and thought, "Wow, I made this."

That feeling of creation was contagious and self-replicating and I knew I had to do it again. Plus the sales team thought it was a great idea, and that it could be something I did every year.

Well, I proudly present [Dis]Connected, Volume 2.

The poets who took part in this book are some of the most amazing people I know. They are talented and their stories so diverse, that I got even more excited about the project when one would show up in my inbox.

The process for the second edition was the same as it was with the first. I asked all ten participating poets to submit three original poems. I then put all their names in a Starbucks mug (hence the awesome illustration by Trista Mateer on the cover), and drew them out one by one.

This is the order that I pulled, so Tyler Knott Gregson would write a short story based on one of Komal Kapoor's poems, and N.L. Shompole would write based on Tyler's, and so on. Poets were told to incorporate a line or two from their assigned poem into their story.

These ten stories will make you feel all the feelings. They'll make you long or love, celebrate what you have, ache for what you've lost, and rejoice in the ope of what is yet to come. The humanity in them is visceral and real and educed me to tears a few times.

These poets are multi-talented—as you're about to find out. Read their work here, then go out and read their poetry. You'll be happy you did.

May you find as much joy in reading this as I did in creating it.

— Michelle Halket, Publisher — Central Avenue

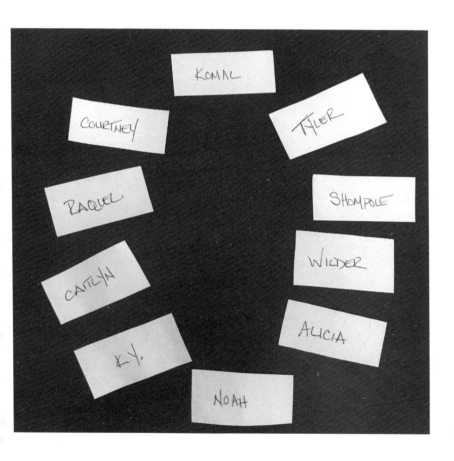

CONTENTS

[DIS]CONNECTED

The Fibers Between Things

Tyler Knott Gregson

Sometimes I can see the fibers between things,
The threads that connect us,
Tie us all together. I can see the light
As it passes over them, as it moves,
Undulates, like it is water and the
Shadow it casts against the sea floor.
Often they stretch tight, creaking and
Threatening snap, often they slacken,
Make large troughs and high peaks,
The sine and the cosine,
The mathematics of it.

I can still them, reach out my hands as if
Conducting, calm their vibrations when excited
They become, when before me stands a breathing thing. A wild one.

I imagine messages sent along the length of them, curling over the
knots
That secure the ends. I whisper as they grow,
As they recede.

Listen, I offer, hear me and hold it like a first
promise, like a vow recited under torchlight,
Orange glowing on the faces of us both:

You are safe with me.

Strangers Tomorrow

N. L. Shompole

*W*ELCOME TO JANUARY HOUSE. THE words tumble out of my mouth so easily, I hardly remember saying them. When I look up, it's to meet a pair of brown, time-faded eyes.

Over the years, I've come to know all the variations of light that eyes can hold. Some eyes are like captured stars, brilliant. Others are memory-worn, the glow washed out like a firefly in the last dance of night.

A hundred thousand eyes. That's how many I have seen, give or take a few. That's why I can tell you what he's hiding when our gazes meet. That's why I can tell you what haunting brought him to our doorstep.

Knowing which madness drives people to us is a matter of experience, and not some technological wonder or witchy-trick, though it has been called both over the years.

Standing in the doorway, backlit by the soft orange glow of the lobby, is a man far older than his years. A grief-stricken man. Ridges crowd the corners of his eyes, outdone only by the war trenches that furrow his brown-skinned forehead. At first guess, I would have pegged him as a man in his twilight years. His shoulders are slightly bowed with age. The only tell otherwise is in his sharp, purposeful steps.

I like him immediately. One, because he doesn't glance over his shoulder to see if anyone has seen him enter the January House, and two, because he does not tuck his head in shame as many others do—as if they had magically appeared on our doorstep.

A doorstep, I might add, that is nearly impossible to happen upon unless you know exactly where you are going.

"How can I help you?" I ask, the words of the script long ago etched into muscle memory.

He stares at me for so long, I begin to question if I actually said the words out loud.

There was a time when there was no script to recite. A time when we didn't work in small, cube-like reserves tucked between the shadows of high-rises. In those days, men and women sought us out at the prime of their lives, not when the world had worn them down to bones, not when pain had soured them on life.

That was before January Corp. came along and changed everything. But even they could not change the need for our existence. We were essential, the way air was essential.

They wanted to replace us with machines at first, but countless trials, experiments, and prototypes soon proved that it was impossible to take us out of the process.

I guess there was something necessary in our DNA, something that even the best scientists and inventors could not parse out. After some time, it became clear that we were the key to everything, that our bodies held some essential component they could not do without, some essential mathematics without which the January Machines were rendered non-functional. But that's not my problem.

What I care about is the man pulling a small, blank, orange card from the pocket of a well-worn suit jacket and sliding it over the counter.

I stand, flicking off *Tausi*, the soap opera I was watching before the man came in. I bring up the appropriate screen, scan the card, and hand it back.

It does not tell me his name. It doesn't need to. Soon, I will know him better than he knows himself.

The man takes the card back, the gesture revealing a faint tremor in his hands. Nerves or worry? I have no idea. Instead, I root around in my mind for the rest of the script and force myself to say it, ignoring how stale the words taste in my mouth.

"This way, sir," I say. "It takes bravery to make such a hard choice. But don't worry; a new beginning is just within reach." The words rattle in my mind like a pebble in a tin can.

Somewhere along the way, the words became a mantra. *A new beginning is just within reach.* Sometimes when I can't sleep, I repeat them over and over and over again until I am lost in the sea of my dreams.

We are in the January Pods when the man finally speaks. He clears his throat, and I see the beginnings of hope bloom in his wizened eyes before it is quickly crowded out by doubt.

He doesn't have to ask the questions. I see them all in his eyes. Will it hurt? What will happen afterwards? What if I want to go back? Is this the right thing to do?

"It doesn't hurt," I reassure him, following the script. The dark orb of the camera's eye in the ceiling is watching me.

In a room far from here, someone in a cubicle is watching everything I do, listening to everything I say, and everything I don't.

I clench my teeth around the words threatening to come out. I don't dare stray from the script. I don't dare tell the man that if I were him, I would keep my memories. If I were him, I would turn around and walk right back out the door, because every pain, every joy I have ever experienced, is worth much more than the second chance he thinks he's getting.

A thick feeling settles in my throat, and it's my turn to hide the tremor in my hands. My gaze lands on his shoes, and the sight is so jarring that I find myself truly looking at him for the first time.

Unlike the rest of his worn but well-cared-for clothes, his shoes are so new that I can see the room reflected in the shine of the leather. The reflection of the orange lamp provides a point of focus that reminds me of a setting sun. I focus on that until my hands stop shaking.

⁓⋎⌁

They don't call it witchcraft anymore. They haven't called it that in a long time, not since January Corp. bought the IPO, promising to invigorate and uplift the communities where they had discovered the memory-soothing tradition, a secret ritual held in the bodies of women for thousands of years. There was a time when women like Mama were the heart of every village across the world. They were the guardians of the things we held most dear, the things that shaped us, our memories, particularly the ones we wanted to forget.

All things change, don't they? Eventually, that essential function became the root for mistrust. Those who were once sought out to help became the accused. What land's history is not scarred by the legacy of witch hunts? Staking, burning, shunning, saving; call it what you like.

Anyway, January Corp. made a killing in the first few years after unveiling the January Pod social platform. It wasn't long before January Houses popped up all over the globe.

"Free Yourself from Yourself." This was their motto. Droves raced to sign up and purchase memberships, drawn by the allure of a clean slate. Freedom. What does that word even mean? Does anyone know?

People nearly died for a chance at gaining a mind unmarred by the mistakes of the past. Unmarked by pain. Funny what people will do for a fresh start.

It wasn't that simple. To erase even a single experience is to fracture. It is to irrevocably change a person. The mind is not like a bone that knits back together after a break. Sure, sometimes it forms new neurons, new pathways. Sometimes it can't. No one knows why.

All that is in the fine print, of course. But when socialite Sydney Chu went on a retreat to the obscure Ndovu Republic to clear her mind and came back a new woman, the whole world went berserk. They wanted it, and they wanted it now.

Who were we—the memory soothers in the days of old, witches in the time after that, the January Women of the new millennium—who were we to refuse?

A small part of the fortune January Corp. made trickled down to women like Mama and me. We were able to build a little nest egg for the future, for when the mania died down and it became like the old days again. Those who wanted to forget were those most scarred by life. Those who could no longer bear remembering. Those whose grief threatened to drown them.

Funny, isn't it, that those who offer the respite are the ones who are unable to forget?

I still remember when the January Man came to our door. I was seven. Mama opened the door to a man in a crisp suit and odd white eyeshade. She invited him into our small sitting room, straightening the crocheted seat covers, turning down the television in the corner before dashing into the kitchen. She came out holding a tray with a jug of juice and one trembling glass balanced on it.

I think I can help you, he said to her after taking a sip of the juice. I remember how he grimaced at the warm, too-sweet taste of it before he set the glass down.

He didn't call it witchcraft when he spoke to Mama. He said words that vaguely sounded like "memory conditioning," the words in his mouth crisp and sharp like the creases of his pressed suit pants.

His hair was shorn short, showcasing a high dark-brown forehead and a soft jaw. When he smiled, his teeth looked like rows of white maize.

I hid behind the kitchen door, listening. *How did you find me?* Mama asked, her voice tired with the burden of keeping secrets.

People still called it witchcraft back then. I remember the first time I heard the word *murogi* thrown at her: We were shopping at a vegetable stand outside the main supermarket in town. It was dusk, and she had just come from work in Nairobi, back aching from sitting too long on stiff *matatu* seats as the driver raced down pothole-ridden roads.

Her accuser was a thin-faced man whose wife had left him shortly after visiting Mama. No, Mama hadn't bewitched her. She had offered her a chance to start afresh, to go back and wipe out everything that had happened after that one crucial decision that had split her life into diverging halves.

Forgetting is a strange thing. If you don't remember something that happened, does it still affect who you are? Does the experience leave its mark on you? Does erasing the memory also wipe out the changes it has wrought on you?

Countless papers have been published in all the top medical journals since the unveiling of the first January Machine.

Shortly after the man appeared on our doorstep, we moved. Mama rented a new apartment close to the January Corp. headquarters in Nairobi. She worked long hours, but she seemed happier, even healthier.

For a long time, it seemed as if things had gotten better, and the hardships of her past started to fade in the way memories sometimes do.

"Are you familiar with our procedures?" I ask the old man. They always say no, even though the only way they could have ended up on our doorstep is by signing up for an account on the January House social platform and attending a week of life counseling before being given the address of a location near them.

"Please sit in the pod and place the helmet over your head." I go over it anyway, zoning out as I direct him.

"The controls on the right armrest will adjust the room settings for comfort. That includes visual, tactile, and auditory settings. The controls on the left will monitor your vitals. Once you are ready, simply say 'begin,' and a set of instructions will appear on the screen inside your helmet."

I pause as he sits down in the orange pod. It adjusts, molding to the contours of his body with a quiet hum.

"You can only do this once," I continue. "Once the scan is complete, you pick the locus you want to return to. Make this decision with care. Once you select 'erase,' you cannot go back."

He lifts the helmet and places it on his head, already lost in the depths of possibilities.

You would think that most people who come to January House come to wipe away memories of past crimes or other, simpler transgressions.

Some do, but in truth, most people that end up on our doorstep come because of lost love. They come because the grief threatens to swallow them whole. They come in search of a life preserver, their last chance to escape a capsizing boat.

After he is settled, I tap on my earpiece and offer the final instructions. "If you agree to the conditions, please sign the consent form."

The data-pad in my hand pings, the sound loud in the cubicle. *I AGREE* fills my screen.

⌁

I have never been called a witch, but I've been called a number of other, far worse things. People do not like what they do not understand. They like it far less when you do not even try to conform to their ideas of what you should be.

The first time I was attacked was after the Camelia North debacle. Camelia was a college student who went to a January House after her boyfriend was killed in a car accident. At nineteen, she was old enough to make her own choices, old enough to sign our dotted line.

She went in a healthy girl with a bright future in front of her and came out a clean slate with no memory of anything. Not her parents, not her name, barely able to speak. Worse, she came out unable to form new memories.

As far as I know, that was the only time it ever happened. No one can truly know what went wrong with her procedure. That was back before they started recording everything. Not that it would have helped anyway.

What we do is beyond technology. Sure, they can hook us up to machines, monitor every synapse that fires in the brain, and try to replicate it. But without us as conductors, nothing happens. The pods are just empty machines. The data is just a bunch of graphs and numbers that make no sense.

I slip into the mirror-pod opposite his cubicle as he slips into his memory-scape. I strap myself in, place the helmet on my head, and welcome the burn as fragile, filament-like mirror-neurons spring to life, growing, extending, searching out their counterparts. When they find me, they latch on with the vigor of a newborn babe finding its mother's breast.

It hurts. It always hurts. Sometimes I welcome the pain, but other times it is a near-debilitating jolt to my entire system.

I gasp, suddenly breathless. The first moments always feel like drowning, and then I am submerged into a midnight sea. It takes a while before my vision adjusts, and I begin to see chains of brightly colored gossamer threads, floating in space. I have always been able to see the fibers between things.

There is a kick, a disturbance, that marks the moment the old man becomes fully aware of the connection between us. I wonder what it is like not to be able to see these threads that tie us to each other. What it is like to be so disconnected.

Listen, I offer, *hear me.* I have said the same words countless times before, but this is the only part of the procedure that still feels new, that still feels open and vulnerable.

It only takes a moment before his whole life is at my fingertips. Each gossamer filament I touch sparks bright, spitting out billions of snapshots of his life, more vibrant and complex than anything man can ever hope to make. I remind myself that I hold his entire life in my hands; everything he has ever experienced is there for me, a stranger, to see.

We are alone in the dark, an orange glow on both our faces. You are safe with me. I say. *You are safe with me.*

The promise washes over him and he relaxes. My body follows suit, falling into the tide of his memories. I only need to gesture at each thread to guide it. I am only here to witness, to navigate, and—at the very last moment—to erase.

Before the end, I will know him better than I know myself. His sorrows will tear at my insides like talons, shredding me. His joys will infuse every part of my being, saturating each cell like a million rising suns.

I sit in my mirror-pod and wait and watch as he drifts through his own memory-scape, reliving the best parts, avoiding the worst. They always avoid the worst.

⠴⠖

When it comes, the memory slams into me and over me like an unseasonal typhoon, pulling me into an undertow.

He is young, mid-thirties or early forties. The memory solidifies, and I see him standing at a bus station early one morning. The sky is more gray than blue, with the faint promise of better weather in the afternoon.

He turns and sees her, and it is like being electrocuted. I feel every nerve in his body light, as if someone plugged him straight into a socket. It feels the way I imagine a lightning strike would feel. This is his locus, the place he wants to return to. But this is the thing that has broken him, the thing he wants to forget.

She stands across the street, a child's hand tucked in her own. Traffic is heavy, cars and *boda-bodas* and *tuk-tuks* zipping this way and that. It is bright and noisy, but he only has eyes for her, for them.

I don't know what it says about people, but the locus is nearly always the same. But this one, this one shatters me in a way nothing has before.

We are in lockstep now, seeing in tandem, rising in tandem. There is a gap in the flow of traffic. She steps out into the road. It is one of those major roads with four lanes. For a moment, the vehicles have stopped. She walks quickly. The cars start moving again, and she starts walking faster, dragging her daughter behind her as she races for the median. There is a wall of traffic, and then a bus. I hear the echo of his words in my own mind. *Too fast. It's coming too fast.*

The bus is moving so quickly the world blurs around it. His hands go up, and I feel the tug on my own arms as if directed by some phantom puppeteer in the shadows.

I feel the burst of adrenalin spreading though his body, making him weightless. I am lightheaded with the suddenness of it all. I feel his foot strike the road, but it is nothing like the kick-in-the-heart force of the bus on her body.

I feel the buckling.

I feel the darkening.

When he reaches her, I feel the shattering.

Numbness spreads, consuming. There is no room for thought, for anything but action.

Somewhere in the dark, a faint light goes on.

I feel the candlelight of hope when he realizes that his daughter, their daughter, is still alive.

I feel concrete on knees like steel hammers as he scoops up his daughter. As he tries to pick up his wife's limp body.

I feel the slow encroaching of grief rising over him. I feel the drowning.

⸙

The Memory Reformatting Procedure takes forty-five minutes. I step out of my pod exactly forty-six minutes after receiving his consent. I can't seem to lose the tremor in my knees.

I pretend I am watching *Tausi* when he walks back into the lobby. The main character's voice drones in the background as he crosses to the reception counter.

"Can I trouble you for some directions to the city?" he asks. His voice is sharp but somehow hollow without the weight of grief to give it shape.

He stands taller, unbowed. The lines on his forehead are smoother. His jacket stretches tight over his shoulders. His trousers are a tad too short. His shoes are the only things that fit him.

You would think witnessing a person's most intimate memories would be the most disturbing part of the whole procedure, but it's not. It's the way they look at me afterwards. When they step out of the January Pods and look at me, it is as if they have never seen me before, as if we are strangers. Except that I know everything about them. I will never be able to forget.

He smiles, but the light doesn't quite reach his eyes. I get the sensation that I am looking at the unmaking of a picture, a photograph

14

developing in reverse.

"Take a left at the end of the street and another left. There is a bus station seventy meters from there. You can't miss it."

Notes on How to Take Flight

N. L. SHOMPOLE

Sometimes the night will refuse to let go of you and your skin will reek of dark things, of sadness, of fear, of flight. Sometimes you will remember how he made you laugh and how it shattered every fence, every barricade, every resistance your heart tried to mount. You will forget things from before, things that cut deep, things that dug trenches inside you, things that taught you how to be scared, how to ache. Sometimes, sometimes you will cry, and the night will open up and the tears will become a torrent / a storm / a flood of all the grief long buried. All the rotten things will rise to the surface, washed out to sea by the rainstorm. Sometimes you will miss things you cannot name, and the ache will be a sharp blade, a fire against the tenderness of memory, of living. One day you will understand that the missing is just missing, that it was never enough to keep you there, it was never enough to make you stay. One day, one day you will learn how to navigate the dark, how to grow feathers. One day you will learn how to take flight.

What the Wild Gave Me

I HATED THAT FEELING, THAT MOMENT IN between sleep and wakefulness when you felt like you were starting to fall. I felt my body jump and wondered if anyone else had noticed. Tarot hadn't moved since we left the terminal over an hour before. She had always been a good traveler, much better than me, anyway. I wished I could be as comfortable as she looked. I hadn't slept for days, and all I wanted was a bed.

The Seattle skyline had faded awhile ago. It was hard leaving a city, never knowing how long it would be until you saw it again. I'd spent most of my life leaving things behind, saying goodbye to friends a little sooner than expected. I never blamed my parents for moving us from state to state every year of my childhood; if anything, it helped me get out of my shell and prepare me for the many seasons of life. Especially this one. Being an only child and the "new kid," my only hope for making friends was to be the outgoing one, the "conversation starter," as Dad called it. Mom said the name River had picked me for a reason: "You're always moving to find your way."

Most of my life had been spent living in big cities. Chicago. Los Angeles. Philadelphia. Seattle was the in-between I hadn't realized my soul needed. The wild was in the distance, but seeing it with my own eyes had brought me closer to myself. And now, I was finding my way to it with a broken heart in one hand and hope in the other.

I leaned my head against the window as I looked out at the expanse of blue stretching in front of me. Thinking about my parents and the love they'd shared for all these years, I couldn't help but wonder where Asher and I had gone wrong. My heart was missing him a little louder that day, maybe because there were more miles between us, or maybe it was the growing number of days that had passed since he said goodbye. Either way, the distance kept widening, and I still didn't know how to heal. It was Sunday, 10:32 a.m. Normally we would still have been in bed for a couple more hours, him with coffee and me with tea, playfully arguing about whose turn it was to let the dog out. Instead, I was on a ferry headed toward San Juan Island because "this is where you find yourself." At least that's what Aunt Henna had told me. That's where her cabin was, in the middle of the woods and a short walk to the sea. I hadn't been there since our family reunion six summers earlier, but I was sure my eyes would find something to fall in love with there. I desperately needed a reason to pick up my camera again.

"Can I pet your dog?"

A doe-eyed girl of maybe six stood in front of me with a slight smile. She wore a knee-length, dark-blue dress with tiny silver crescents, and I liked her right away; I loved anything that had to do with the moon and its phases. She wore her hair braided and messy, just like me, only hers was dark brown and reached down to her waist. A pair of binoculars hung from a strap around her neck.

"Of course you can. I'm sure she would love to get out of her carrier for a little while."

"What's her name?" the girl asked.

"This is Tarot. Why don't you sit down next to me, and I'll put her in your lap."

Tarot sniffed the little girl's face and licked her ear.

"Oh, be careful! She likes to chew on earrings," I said.

The girl's smile spread across her face. "She looks just like a fox!"

"She really does, doesn't she?" I replied.

People often mistook Tarot for a fox or a small coyote. When Asher and I had adopted her over a year before, the people at the shelter weren't sure what she was, but they were positive that she had some husky in her. We'd meant to have one of those DNA tests done, but time got away from us . . . in more ways than one.

"My name is Isla. What's your name?"

"I'm River. It's so nice to meet you. I like those binoculars you have there. What are you hoping to see with them?" I said with a grin.

"Thanks!" Her excitement was palpable. "We're going whale watching!"

She reminded me of myself when I was a child. Extroverted and curious. She had dumped her gold-colored bag on the floor, the open flap exposing a black Field Notes notebook, several patterned pencils, and bubble gum. The memory of simpler days hit me, when the world seemed so big, and all I ever needed was a journal and an open window. But here I was, a twenty-five-year-old ex-fiancée with my entire life inside of a duffel bag, looking for a place to call home again.

"Good morning. This is your captain speaking. We will be reaching Friday Harbor in the next twenty minutes, so please be sure to gather all of your belongings and prepare for arrival. Thank you for traveling on the Washington State Ferry. We hope you enjoy your visit."

My visit. I didn't know how long I would be staying on the island. Aunt Henna was backpacking in Europe for six weeks to "clear her head" and had asked me to look after her cabin and bookstore while she was away, insisting I could stay as long as I wanted. Her invitation was more than welcome because I needed something, anything, to keep me busy. Staying in Seattle would only remind me of everything I had lost.

"Thank you for letting me pet Tarot. She's so cute."

"You're welcome. I hope you have fun whale watching with your family today."

"By the way, I love your pictures," Isla said.

"Pictures?" I asked.

She pointed to different places on her arms, and I realized she was talking about my tattoos. Asher and I had planned to get matching ones on our wrists after the wedding.

"Oh, these pictures. Thanks!"

The island loomed a few hundred yards ahead, blanketed in a thick fog along the tree line. There was a storm coming. This was the kind of weather that I loved more than anything and was the reason I'd moved from Arizona to the rainy Pacific Northwest. I felt an affinity for the rain. It seemed to wash everything clean, even me. The rain seemed to know where to find me when I needed it most.

....

Fir trees lined the winding roadway. It seemed every imaginable shade of green existed on this island. Raindrops snaked their way down the window of the taxi, hesitating, then moving quickly, then stopping once more before becoming a part of the next one in their path—now a bigger, stronger drop. The symbolism was not lost on me. I pressed my fingers to the coolness of the window. Tarot was scared of the wiper blades, but their rhythm made me sleepy.

"What brings you to town?" the driver asked.

"Oh . . . I'm just visiting family." I hesitated to share more. I didn't want him to know that I was here alone and that Aunt Henna had left. But did I really need to worry about things like that here? I'd never heard about anything bad happening on San Juan Island. It was small and quaint, a twenty-minute drive across the entire island from the ferry terminal.

"This is it," he announced, flashing me a smile in the rearview mirror.

The cabin sat on a hill and was surrounded by native wildflowers. A large vegetable-and-herb garden rested under the front bay window. There was a wooden sign sticking out of the ground that read, "What the wild gave me."

"Yes, this is definitely it. Thank you so much."

The property was even more beautiful than I remembered. Aunt Henna's Instagram posts didn't do it justice. I hefted my bag and Tarot's carrier from the backseat of the cab, following the cobblestone walkway and admiring the koi pond and the large Buddha statue wrapped in mala beads. Every second step along the path was dotted with an abalone shell placed carefully along the edge, each with a white votive candle resting inside. I could still picture the photos my aunt had shared of all the candles lit by her front door in celebration of the rising full moon. Aunt Henna was the person in my family I'd always looked up to most and the reason for my love of the moon. She was a free spirit who found beauty in everything, and I'd always wanted to be like her.

She had texted the night before, telling me the key was under the mat. That should have been my first indication that I didn't need to worry about safety here. After all, wasn't that the first place everyone looked?

"Tarot, come here!" The dog was up to her neck in the koi pond. "Get over here! That's all I need is for something to die within the first five minutes of our stay."

The scent of peppermint and cedar hit me the moment I opened the door: palo santo sticks. An aching emptiness spread though my chest. Aunt Henna had mailed me a package of them, along with some crystals from her shop, for my birthday, explaining that palo could heal anything. I believed that, but right now, the smell reminded me of home. Our home. The one that I would never get back.

There were a set of keys and a credit card on the kitchen island, along with a note:

Welcome, River and Tarot! Here are the keys to the car and bookstore. The shop opens tomorrow at 10:00, and Rowan will meet you there at 9:30 to fill you in. Use this card (the pin is 3377) to get gas and groceries. We have a spot in town called Kings Market where you can get everything you need. It's only two blocks north of the bookstore.

Send me an email if you have to get ahold of me. I don't think my phone will work. In case of emergency, I left my neighbor Sama's number on the side of the fridge. Please make yourself at home, and thank you so much for your help. I'll see you in mid-September. Have fun! Oh! If you could also water the plants once a week, that would be great!

Love,

Aunt Henna

P.S. The koi food is in the pantry on the lower left shelf next to the bird feed.

Plants? Really? Asher had been responsible for any plant life in our loft for a reason; he used to joke that I had a black thumb. It was like a greenhouse in here. Maybe I should call him and ask for advice. He probably would answer. But then again, I'd promised myself I wouldn't call or text. I'd lasted almost a full week. I didn't want to break that record.

I shook it off and walked slowly around the cabin. Vaulted ceilings came down at a deep angle where a row of skylights sat. It was a small two-bedroom home, but the openness of the space and endless natural light made it seem much larger. Aunt Henna's style was bohemian and eclectic. The wooden floors were layered with oversized rugs, and the walls were covered in original art pieces she had collected on her travels. I was particularly drawn to the hallway, which showcased African carved masks and Indian tapestries. I had never seen so many candles or crystals in all my life, or at least not outside of a shop that sold them. They flooded every flat surface. Candle. Crystal. Plant. Repeat. It was an organized mess. Kind of like me, I mused. Carved teak tables and singing bowls were the focal point in the guest bedroom. Feathers, bones, driftwood, and other found objects from the ocean were placed nicely inside flat shadow-box frames on the floor next to the daybed. I lay down on it and gazed toward the farthest side of the room, where two French doors opened to a lofted patio facing the back of the property. This was where the forest met the Salish Sea. It was a beautiful view. Like a postcard. Like a dream.

....

It was 9:30 a.m., and the smell of old books brought me back to the days I'd spent with Mom in the study. I'd lost and found myself in her favorite stories, but she always told me that Aunt Henna had an even better collection. The bookstore was tiny but charming, packed from floor to ceiling with shelves that overflowed into the narrow aisles. Small bowls were arranged in a line on a long table by the window, each filled with different crystals and stones. A vintage card-catalog cabinet fit snugly in the corner. Each drawer bore a label in Aunt Henna's handwriting, describing what was inside. "Incense. Palo. Spell candles. Tarot cards." Her bookstore was like an extension of her cabin.

"And of course there are more plants for me to kill," I said under my breath, glancing around the shop.

A familiar song played in the background—Of Monsters and Men had long been one of my favorite bands. Happiness swept over me for a moment as I remembered the summer Asher surprised me with tickets to Coachella. He never cared for their music much, but insisted he liked them because I did. I followed the black-and-white hexagonal tiles to the back of the shop.

"You must be River!"

A tall and slender twenty-something man with dark hair stood behind an old-fashioned cash register, counting change. The space was furnished with a few oversized velvet chairs and side tables.

"And you must be Rowan," I said with subtle enthusiasm.

"Would you like some coffee or tea?"

"Tea would be great. English Breakfast if you have it."

There was something magical about this place. It was no wonder Aunt Henna had called this island home for so long. I grew up thinking I needed to be a city girl to be successful and "make it" in life, but after college I grew disillusioned with it, the rush, the never-ending noise, the stress of trying to keep up. Not that Seattle was a huge city, but being here on San Juan Island made me feel different, like I could breathe.

I noticed a stack of local newspapers on the table beside me. "Southern Resident Orcas Nearing Extinction." The news stories about the decline in the orca population had seemed so far removed from the relevance of my urban life.

"It's sad, isn't it? Nothing should have to starve to death," Rowan said, handing me my tea.

"It's awful," I replied quietly, embarrassed to tell him I had no idea why they were starving.

"Yeah, and it's such an easy solution: let the salmon come back to their breeding grounds in the rivers, and the whales will be just fine. You know they don't eat seals, so they depend on the salmon. It's all connected, and we ridiculous humans can't seem to see that!"

I thought of the whales, the salmon, the rivers. Their connection to each other. I must have looked a little wistful, and Rowan gently interrupted my thoughts.

"The shop is open from ten until four every day and is closed on Sundays," he said.

Rowan went on to say he would manage the café, and I would oversee the rest of the shop, making sure it stayed organized. Aunt Henna maintained a log of all the used books donated as well as the ones that sold, and also ordered new crystals and other items when the inventory got low. I would take care of all of those things while she was away. Rowan offered to care for the plants and flowers outside. I was grateful for that, knowing my lack of ability in plant care, but hesitant to let him know it.

"Every Saturday, Freya, our local psychic, comes in for a few hours."

"Oh! A psychic?" I was excited. I'd had my cards read after my senior year of college, but I'd never met a real psychic before.

"She's really good, and the locals love her. Henna is hoping that having her at the shop will attract the tourists. We don't want to have another bad year like we did last year; if we do, we may have to close the doors."

Aunt Henna had never mentioned that the store wasn't doing well. She was rather proud though; she and Mom were alike in that way. Always willing to help others, but never asking for anything in return. I was happy to be here, despite the circumstances, and even more grateful that she'd asked me to help while she was away. And as the August breeze came through the propped-open door, I smiled for what felt like the first time in weeks.

....

The sound of the orcas breaching the ocean's surface had become my favorite part of these kayaking trips. To see them from a distance was one thing, but to hear them was simply beautiful.

"Did you get a shot of that?" Rowan asked. I guess my excitement was contagious.

"Yes! It was perfect timing."

The rush of it would never get old. We had spent every Sunday of the last month coming to this spot, and our gentle friends came to see us each time. I wasn't able to identify them by name like Rowan, but all that mattered to me was that my life felt like it had purpose again. I'd spent the past few years building my photography business, taking photos of everyone else's happy moments, completely forgetting to capture my own. It was nice to give back to myself, but also to the island. Rowan was actively involved in the movement to bring awareness to the ailing southern resident orcas, and introduced me to some of his friends that were trying to do the same. I offered to help where I could, taking photographs of the whales during our Sunday rows and selling prints in the shop to help raise money for both the bookstore and the orca fund.

"How much longer do you think you'll stay on the island?"

Aunt Henna would be back from her trip in two weeks, and I wasn't sure what I was going to do next. I wondered if she'd meant it when she said I could stay for as long as I wanted.

"I'm not really sure, I guess. There isn't anywhere else that's calling to me."

Mom and Dad had told me I was welcome to come stay with them in Tennessee, but something about moving back in with them didn't feel right. Sure, I was only twenty-five, and plenty of people my age lived with their parents, but I really didn't want to. Besides, the island was starting to feel like home.

Today was the day Asher and I would have been leaving for our honeymoon. Kylee had texted me yesterday to say she was thinking of me, and told me yet again that I was better off without someone who didn't know how lucky they were to have me. She was so sweet, that girl. My best friend since high school, Kylee was gregarious and outgoing, opinionated to a fault and fiercely protective of those she loved. Maybe she was right, but I had a lot of unanswered questions about the way things had ended. Asher and I were together four years, and then one day he'd said, "I don't love you anymore." I'd been devastated, and completely surprised. I wondered if today's date meant anything to him.

"Look at that sunset. Isn't it the most amazing thing you have ever seen?" Rowan's observation interrupted my reverie.

Trumpeter swans honked up ahead as the sun made its descent. The sky was painted in pinks at the horizon, blending upward into shades of indigo and slate.

"It really is," I said, looking up at the emerging stars.

"Oh, and the moon!" he exclaimed, pointing his hand toward the sky. "It's going to be a full one tonight."

It was the first full moon since I'd left Seattle. It gazed at me, round and wise, telling me I was exactly where I needed to be.

....

I was never one for routines. Since birth, my days had been haphazard; my mom told me I'd never slept when I was supposed to, never ate when others did, and always wanted to play when others were working. Oh sure, I conformed when I needed to, went to school, work, the gym, but it never felt natural, that forced routine. But living here and going to the bookshop nearly every day for the past six weeks had shifted things. Without an alarm, I woke up at the same time each morning, took Tarot on a walk in the woods for an hour to let her explore and get her energy out, made myself a cup of tea, and journaled before getting ready to leave for the day. I'd come straight home after the shop closed, make myself dinner, and eat by the wood-burning stove with a book in my hand. Then, after washing my face and brushing my teeth, I'd cry myself to sleep, wondering how I'd made it through another day. I had fallen into a pattern without even realizing it.

....

The smell of sautéed vegetables filled the kitchen, and Tarot was begging at my feet for food. I tossed a slice of red pepper across the room for her to fetch, and put a few corn tortillas on the skillet to warm while the vegetables sat in the pan a little longer. I inhaled deeply; I loved when the onions got brown and crispy at the edges.

The doorbell rang, startling both of us, and Tarot started barking.

"Tarot, be quiet!" I scolded.

No one ever came to the door except the mail carrier, but he had already been here today, and Aunt Henna wasn't due to return from Europe until tomorrow afternoon.

"Tarot, come here!" I picked her up and opened the door.

"Hey," he said, staring at me with hesitation.

I stared back at him, Tarot fighting with all her might to get out of my arms.

"Tarot, my puppy! I've missed you so much!"

Tarot jumped at his legs, whining with excitement. At least one of us was happy to see him.

"What are you doing here?" I asked sharply.

"Do you think you can invite me in first?"

The smoke alarm echoed loudly down the hallway.

"Oh, shoot!"

I ran into the kitchen and took the tortillas off the stove.

"Taco Tuesday, huh?" he said with a smirk.

"How did you even know where to find me?"

"Your aunt's address was on our spreadsheet for the wedding invitations."

Tarot was licking his face like crazy. Who did he think he was, showing up on my doorstep after what he did to me?

"Oh, how convenient," I snapped.

"I tried texting you to see how you were, but you didn't answer."

He was right. I'd ignored him a few times this past week. I knew better than to respond and get sucked into the black hole of text messages, which would only lead me to wonder why he had taken so long to reply, and then I'd question the meaning behind every word he wrote once he finally did.

"Me not responding isn't an invitation for you to just show up uninvited."

"I know it isn't, but I needed to see you. I miss you, and I don't know how to say this in any other way except just to say it. I love you, more than I could ever express. I made a mistake—a huge mistake— when I left you, and all I want is to fix it and make all of this better. I want to be us again."

He paused for what seemed like forever. I had no words to offer. I was too upset to say anything.

"I'm not asking you to answer me right now. I'm just asking you to think about it."

Silence found its way between us again.

"Can you please say something?" he asked.

"Asher. I don't know what to say. I'm shocked. All I've wanted was for you to call and say exactly what you just said. I waited for weeks to hear these words from you, and it took everything in me not to call and beg for you to find your way back to us. You broke me in ways I never thought possible, and I'm finally finding a way to pick those pieces back up again."

I held back my tears, but I could feel the flood coming and I didn't want him to see it. He came in to hug me. I stepped back.

"I can't do this right now. I need to think about all of this. There's so many questions I still need answers to, I don't even know where to begin."

"Okay, River," he said quietly, "I understand."

"Are you hungry?" I asked. I was starving and on the verge of a migraine.

He smiled. "Yes. I've missed our taco Tuesdays."

....

Shades of gray carried on for miles and miles. The rain had been falling for days and in some strange way, I felt as though the sky was crying with me. Asher had gone back to Seattle yesterday, and everything still felt so uncertain.

I hated for Aunt Henna to see me so unhappy, but having her back home helped dull the ache.

"What's on your mind, sweetheart?" Aunt Henna asked.

I wondered what gave it away. Maybe the fact that I'd counted the change in the cash drawer eleven times over.

"Oh, ya know, just contemplating this crazy life of mine," I said.

"Well, the guest bedroom is yours until it's ready to kick you out," she said jokingly.

"Thank you so much, Aunt Henna. I really appreciate everything you've done for me."

"Honestly, River. It's the least I can do. You've helped the bookstore in ways I hadn't thought of. You gave it life and purpose again. Not to mention all the time and dedication you've given so selflessly for the orcas. The island is a part of you now, and you—you are a part of it, too. That kind of bond lasts forever, no matter where you and your heart may land."

San Juan Island had become my home, and the thought of leaving it all behind made me feel empty. I'd lived in many places throughout my life, but there was never one that spoke to me the way the island did.

"You should meet with Freya when she comes in this afternoon. Maybe she can help you find the answers you're looking for."

The idea of talking with the psychic both excited me and made me feel anxious, but I was desperate for direction, and anything seemed better than nothing right now.

"That's a good idea," I said, looking at the schedule. "She has an opening at twelve thirty."

I penciled myself in and watered the plants to pass the time, while Rowan got the café ready for the day. I had gotten rather good at the whole plant thing lately and had managed to kill only three of them while Aunt Henna was away.

·········

The psychic reading room was compact and had the perfect amount of light and dark, with a candle as the only source of illumination. It smelled sweet, like rosewater and lavender with a touch of patchouli. A round glass table with two golden wingback chairs sat in the center of the room on an oriental rug. Freya had a gentle spirit about her. She was an older woman, originally from New Orleans, who'd come to live with her sister who had recently fallen ill.

"Sit down, sweet child," she said kindly.

She touched my hands and closed her eyes. We sat in silence for a moment. She began spinning the ring on my index finger. It was a gift from my mother before I left for college, and had originally belonged to my great-grandmother. I never took it off.

"This is very special to you and holds more meaning than you realize," Freya said as she removed the ring from my finger. It was silver with a bird on top that had a small fire opal in its wing. She put it in her palm and motioned for me to place both of my hands around hers. "When the things we love most leave this earth, they come back to help guide us home." She paused for a moment, then continued. "Sometimes the night will refuse to let go of you and your skin will reek of dark things, of sadness, of fear, of flight. Sometimes you will remember how he made you laugh and how it shattered every fence, every barricade, every resistance your heart tried to mount.

You will forget things from before, things that cut deep, things that dug trenches inside you, things that taught you how to be scared, how to ache. Sometimes, sometimes you will cry, and the night will open up and the tears will become a torrent. A storm. A flood of all the grief long buried. All the rotten things will rise to the surface, washed out to sea by the rainstorm. Sometimes you will miss things you cannot name, and the ache will be a sharp blade, a fire against the tenderness of memory, of living. One day you will understand that the missing is just missing, that it was never enough to keep you there, it was never enough to make you stay. One day, one day you will learn how to navigate the dark, how to grow feathers. One day you will learn how to take flight."

I sat silently with my eyes on her. A tear ran down my cheek, and I could feel the rest of the storm coming.

"Let it go. Let it go," she whispered.

I had been drowning for so long that I'd forgotten what it felt like to keep my head above water. Asher had broken pieces of me that I thought could never break, yet despite it all, I was still here, fighting to find my way back home.

"There is so much that needs to be saved here, and it's the only place that knows how to save me," I said through my tears. "All along, I've been holding the answer, and I just didn't know how to see it."

I sat back against the chair and breathed a sigh of relief. Freya reached up and touched my face.

"That's the thing about being one with the wild; you're always growing."

the thing about time

WILDER

i remember the days
i was unafraid of change,
when i was just a young girl
looking out of car windows
waving goodbye to a city
that didn't want me to go,
but knew i couldn't stay.

i closed my eyes
and everything looked the same,
i opened them knowing it wasn't.
i always saw hope in the distance.
another trip around the sun—
a memory i couldn't hold,
but one that always knew where
to find me.

and that's the beautiful thing about time,

it helps us forget what we may have missed
and remember everything we never wanted to leave.

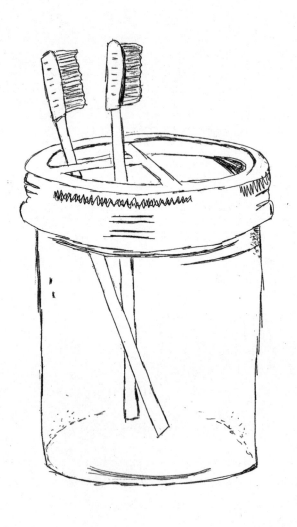

The Fourth Saturday

i closed my eyes
and everything looked the same,
i opened them knowing it wasn't.

OR THE FOURTH SATURDAY IN A ROW, I don't want to wake up. I will my eyes to remain closed, to ignore the light leaking in through that one bent slat in the blinds I keep meaning to pop back into place. I stick my hand underneath my pillow and find my phone. 11:02 a.m. We are officially four Saturdays removed. I want to puke. I want to sleep. I am pretty sure I still want to die. You know, all normal things for a seventeen-year-old to feel during summer break.

For the fourth Saturday in a row, the house is quiet and doesn't smell of bacon. There are no sounds of a sizzling pan or of pots clanging together, or my father cursing under his breath. Bacon and eggs on Saturday mornings was a tradition in my house as far back as I can remember. Breakfast was Dad's thing. It drove Mom mad that my twin sister, Harper, and I liked his bacon best. In reality, Harper and I believed their bacon tasted the same, but the experience of Dad cooking far eclipsed Mom's quiet execution of the same task. Dad seemed to have the heat too high, so it would splatter everywhere. Grease speckled the oven, the backsplash, the floor. Then we would sit down as a family and eat together, listening to Mom bitch (albeit good-naturedly) about how messy a cook my father was. The banter that ensued was why we preferred Dad's breakfast.

Those mornings seem so far away now, almost like they didn't exist in the first place. Like I dreamed it all up. I know they were real, though, because sometimes when I walk by the deli, I am greeted by the smell, and I cry.

For the fourth Saturday in a row, I pad down the hall, one sock on, one sock off, and head toward the bathroom. My parents' bedroom door is ajar, enough for me to see my mother still sleeping. Up until four Saturdays ago, outside of dozing off on the couch with Dad during a John Wayne movie, I had never seen my mother actually asleep. Not once. She was always up early, walking the dogs, or making sure her birdfeeders were amply filled and not destroyed by the squirrels. She woke Harper and me up every morning for school, already showered, dressed, and smiling.

"Honeybuns! It's a quarter to seven! Wake up!"

Two Saturdays ago, the doctor prescribed Mom Xanax to help with everything, but after trying them, she flushed the rest. My mother thought numbing herself during this time would only come back and bite her in the ass in the long run.

When Grandma died last year, my mother asked my father to pull into the CVS on the way home from the cemetery.

"Don't you want to go home, Mel? Relax? You've had a long

week," Dad softly suggested.

"You never bring death home," Mom said, already unbuckling her seatbelt. "Come on, girls. Let's go in. We need to drop our death off here." The three of us walked around CVS for ten minutes while Dad waited patiently in the car. We bought M&Ms just because.

Four Saturdays ago, when we were coming home from that same cemetery, I noticed we passed the CVS without a second thought and just headed right back home. Even Mom knew there was no possible way to drop off death this time. This loss was going to stick. Like gum matted in hair.

I pee and notice my urine is dark orange. I'm dehydrated, but I'm not thirsty. I flush and make my way to the sink. I reach for my toothbrush.

Mom has always said that if you want to truly see the passage of time, look no further than the toothbrush holder. We were a family of four, so for most of our lives, there were four toothbrushes. Their number would occasionally fluctuate: Sometimes there'd be two—just Mom's and Dad's—when Harper and I were at camp. Other times, there'd be three, like when Dad went to D.C. for work. But it always landed back at four. Four hearts, four mouths, four toothbrushes. Four.

Now, four Saturdays removed, I notice that there are only three toothbrushes resting in the glass cup. When did that happen? Who was strong enough to dispose of it? To accept that that toothbrush would never be used again? People talk about how hard the holidays become, and cleaning out bedrooms, and closing out bank accounts, but no one really talks about what the living do with the toothbrush of someone who passes away. I run back to the toilet and puke.

The undeniable sound of vomit spraying into a toilet wakes my mother.

"Are you okay, Gianna?" she asks through the door. She tries the handle, but the door is locked.

"Yes," I lie. All we do is lie to each other lately. I can see through the gap under the door that she is still standing outside. I concede. "I noticed the toothbrush was gone."

"It was time," she says.

I return to the sink and brush my teeth again. I enter the kitchen and find my mother and father sitting on opposite ends of the kitchen island. Dad is reading the paper. Mom is tracing the marble with her finger, much like the way children map out images in clouds. Will we ever feel like a family again?

There's never been a time when I didn't have a sister. People say that you come into this world alone and you leave this world alone. But that wasn't the case for Harper and me. I came into this world with my sister. Literally. Technically, she was a minute older than me, which is barely anything, but she never let me forget it and would enforce her right as the older sibling to blow out her birthday candles first. Turns out, she held the authority to die first, too.

Harper and I used to be so mad at our parents for not making us identical. She had light brown hair, and mine is raven black. She had hazel eyes while I got the luck of the draw and have emerald. She was two inches taller. She is now spoken of in past tense; I remain present.

We couldn't get over the fact that we weren't like all the twins in the movies we were obsessed with watching. We wanted so badly to be identical, to pull off the antics that only identical twins could, like tricking our teachers or softball coaches. Young logic convinced us it was our parents' fault for not trying hard enough.

Four Saturdays removed, I have never been so relieved not to share the face of my sister. My general existence is hard enough on my parents right now. When you lose one kid, you have one left. Not with twins. We were one. But at least my parents don't have to look their dead kid in the face every day. And at least I am not greeted by my dead sister every time I look in the mirror.

I kiss both my parents on the cheek, then look at the front door. The alarm is still blinking red, so I know neither of them have ventured outside yet. I feel sudden relief, as if I had been holding my breath.

The summer between junior and senior year of high school, teenagers across the country are greeted daily by glossy card-stock invites from colleges and universities. They are addressed to us, not our parents, a marketing ploy that works because it makes us feel grown up. Four Saturdays ago, the same day as Harper's funeral, Harper and I each received two college visit packets.

HARPER RICCI
█████CLAIRIDGE CT
GLEN RIDGE, NJ 07028

GIANNA RICCI
█████CLAIRIDGE CT
GLEN RIDGE, NJ 07028

Before Harper died, we couldn't wait to visit colleges. We had even started this past school year. A few months before everything, Dad took us to New York to check out Fordham and NYU. We didn't know where we would end up, but Harper and I knew it would be the same school.

Harper wanted to be a writer. She kept journals her whole life. We were never allowed to read them. Unsurprisingly, that was the first thing I did once it dawned on me that her belongings were no longer hers.

Four Saturdays removed, beating my parents to the mail has become a game of sorts. A game with really high stakes. I disarm the alarm and peek outside. I hear splashing and laughing coming from a nearby neighbor's yard. I see birds flying overhead. I wish my bones were hollow, too, so I could escape with ease. I grab a stack of mail. I fan through it and pull out the poison. I leave behind the water bill and the Costco flyer.

It's not enough to just throw away Harper's mail; I have to call the college admissions offices and alert them that she died. I've learned they then mark her as "deceased" in their databases, so the mail stops. I wonder if they do it to save on postage or to keep the air in parents' lungs. Parents shouldn't have to make these calls. I'll call Monday. I'm now a pro at navigating a college's phone prompts.

When I return from the foyer, my mother is pouring food into the dogs' bowls, and I hear the shower burst to life. Last Saturday, my dad didn't shower until 3:00 p.m. The Saturday before that, he didn't shower at all. Four Saturdays ago, he showered early and put on a suit I found the next day in the garbage can near our garage.

My first instinct was to pull the suit out of the trash. To have it washed and put away in a safe place. I thought maybe one day my dad would regret throwing out the outfit he wore to his daughter's wake and funeral. That's when I would swoop in and present him with his suit. It was covered in wet coffee grounds and had already begun to smell like the rest of the garbage. I rummaged through the pockets and found balled-up tissues and wrappers from cough drops. I decided to leave it in the garbage.

Italians attend a lot of funerals. Not because we die at a faster rate, but because if we met you even once, we will go pay our respects. At least, that's the case in my family. Open casket, closed casket, urn, no body at all, we will go. I am only seventeen, and I have been to more wakes than I can count. Two years ago, my uncle's neighbor's thirty-seven-year-old daughter died. Car accident. Closed casket. When Harper asked our mother why we had to go, especially since it was on a Saturday night and we'd never met this woman, my mother said, "Because you don't go for the dead. You go for the living. They're the ones who need comfort."

I wonder how many people were dragged to Harper's wake under those pretenses. It was an open casket. She looked like she was sleeping.

I decide I want to wear Harper's distressed black sweatshirt she bought around Christmas at Zara at the Menlo Park Mall. I head back upstairs and make my way to her room. The door is shut. When we were growing up, my parents had a strict "no closed door" rule, but now her room remains closed off at all times. Death rewrites rules.

I open the door slowly, hearing every click of the glass knob. I look in first, as if someone or something will jump out at me. Her bed is made. The air still smells a bit sour, even though the carpet and everything have been professionally cleaned.

Four weeks and four days ago, we found Harper in her bed, one leg under the covers, one leg hanging off. Bile outlined her mouth, and she was cold. Still, Dad ran to the bathroom for the Narcan. The medics came to tell us what we already knew.

Once she was taken away, Mom cleaned her sheets, made her bed, then shut the door. I am positive she had no intention of ever stepping foot in that room again. Two Saturdays ago, Dad went into her room, maybe to find the car charger he lent her or maybe just to cry, and discovered a long-spoiled glass of milk on her nightstand. I heard him gag, but I don't know if it was because of the smell.

Harper loved whole milk, the full-fat kind. To me, it's like drinking butter, and I used to always get on her about liking to drink it straight, even without cookies. I felt a weird comfort in knowing the last thing she drank was something she loved. Between the stale air in the room and the summer heat that relentlessly beats through the windows on that side of house, the milk, ironically, took on the smell of death. We opened the windows and had the carpet and walls cleaned. I cried, because I knew all her fingerprints were being erased.

Now I don't know if I still smell the milk, or if it is in my head. I finger through her closet, my back to her bed, which I can't bring myself to sit on. Harper had a habit of hanging clothes back up that she had already worn. A huge pet peeve of Mom's, who believed you should wash something once you wore it, even if it was just for a few hours. A few days before Harper died, she wore the Zara sweatshirt, and if I knew my sister, I know she didn't wash it.

I find it and press the fabric to my face. It smells like her. Faintly. How did we get here?

We grew up in a home surrounded by love. We took family vacations to the Jersey Shore, and dinner was at six thirty every evening. Dad helped us with homework, and Mom was a fixture at our school. Harper and I were Girl Scouts, athletes, and had a tight-knit group of shared friends. We had a nine o'clock curfew weeknights and had to have the car back in the driveway by midnight on weekends.

It was all very cookie-cutter, mundane, even. Some would think made up, like a television sitcom. We were a family that got along. That liked being together. As a joke, Dad would yell, "Goodnight, John-Boy!" to us before retreating to his bedroom, referencing *The Waltons,* an old TV show he loved.

Even toward the end, Harper tried her hardest to remain part of the unit. She wrote us letters from Florida, promising things would get back to normal again. I was so happy when she returned home. My sister was my best friend. Is? Was? Is?

Four Saturdays removed, social media is no longer a landmine of sadness or triggers, though messages and photos are still trickling in on Instagram. Harper's social media accounts have become shrines, something unique to my generation. Harper's last post was a photo of the two of us, our legs dangling in our pool around the Fourth of July. We looked happy, even though I know we weren't right. We were so very scared. The photo has collected over a thousand "likes"; most people clicked the heart after she died.

I visit the funeral-home website. It's something I've done nearly every day since the services. I type in Harper's name and click on a photo of her face. In June, we took our senior photos. Harper won't graduate high school now, but we used her senior photo on her prayer card, in the obituary, and on this site. "Hey, we paid for the photos already, might as well put them to use," my father had managed to joke at the time, though no one laughed. I scroll down and read the condolences.

I wrote one on the very day the page went live, just two days after she died. I wonder if time will one day cushion my memory of the utter pain and confusion I felt.

It's nearly twelve thirty, and I am supposed to meet my friend Katie at Montclair Bread Company. Katie was also a friend of Harper's. Her grandfather is in the late stages of Alzheimer's and has moved in with her family. That, coupled with the death of Harper, has taken a toll on her. No one's life is easy. We decided the other day to grab coffee and watch our sadness swirl in it like cream.

Katie recently described her grandfather's early battle, before Alzheimer's completely took over, in a way that made me think of my sister and her disease. Katie said that some days, she would see her grandfather and he would recognize her immediately. His memory would be sharp, and he would remember how the favorite summer of his life smelled of citronella torches. He could name his old teachers, his favorite priest from St. Lucy's in Newark, and all six of his grandchildren.

As his disease progressed, those good visits became fewer and farther between. Katie would see no life behind his eyes. He would look at her as though she were a stranger, and in his mind, she was. Soon, he could not live on his own and had to move in with his family, a family he could no longer recognize. Eventually, all of his memories prior to his disease disappeared.

At the end of my sister's life, that's how I imagine she felt. There were lucid moments with Harper. She would seem like herself and laugh so hard she would snort. But then the very next day, sometimes the next minute, she would be gone again. Until that afternoon four Saturdays ago, when we said goodbye to her forever.

Four Saturdays later, I walk into Montclair Bread and scan the small space for Katie. She's always late. I approach the counter and am greeted by a cashier who doesn't know I vomited this morning, or that I am wearing my dead twin's unwashed shirt.

"Hi! How are you?" she asks.

"Fine," I lie. She doesn't wait for me to tell her the truth.

"What can I get for you today?"

My sister.

My sister.

My sister.

My sister.

"A large iced caramel macchiato with soy milk," I say.

I'm (Not) Fine

Alicia Cook

My throat's collecting dust,
I haven't sung in months.
So overwhelmed by what I need to do
that my to-do list goes untouched.

I can't hold this pose forever.
My legs are starting to tremble.
It's so damn hard to measure up.

I have scrapes on these knees from prayin' too hard,
and scrapes on my heart from stayin' too long.

Oh, I'm broken,
even dreams take their toll and
I need to regain focus.
Goals come with strings,
and when I say I'm tired
you don't get what I mean.

I'm only human;
runnin' on fumes and
sobbing at red lights.

I'm only human;
payin' my dues and
losing all my might.

I'm only human;
lyin' to myself,
sayin' I'm alright.

I'm feelin' the worst pain.
Just trying to save face.
Sitting in therapy wondering why
I keep getting in my own way.

I am a mosaicked woman,
making choices a bit crooked.
Doing things I shouldn't do.

I have aches in my brain from wonderin' too hard,
and aches in my feet from wanderin' too long.

Oh, I'm broken;
even dreams take their toll and
I need to regain focus.
Goals come with strings,
and when I say I'm tired
you don't get what I mean.

I'm only human;
runnin' on fumes and
sobbing at red lights.

I'm only human;
payin' my dues and
losing all my might.

I'm only human;
lyin' to myself
sayin' I'm alright.

Make Choices a Bit Crooked

NOAH MILLIGAN

THE KEY TO MAKING A PROSTHETIC EYE is the mold. You have to get it just right. If you mess it up, the eye can create discomfort. It will burrow deep down inside the socket, jostling against the tissue, irritating it. At first, it might just seem like an irritant. An itch. Something that can be scratched away, the body getting used to something new, something foreign invading it. Soon, surely, the body will accept it. It's just got to adapt, overcome. The human body, after all, is a resilient thing. It can be gashed open with barbed wire, flesh torn, blood spilled, but platelets will rush to the wound, stop the bleeding, and skin cells will multiply and coagulate into scar tissue, even more resilient than before. It truly is a remarkable thing, the human body, but it isn't indestructible. Perhaps there is a tiny aberration in the mold, just a minute sliver of imperfection, imperceptible to the naked eye. It can rub against the socket tissue, rub it raw, rub it continuously until the cells weaken and the skin begins to erode. Eventually, it'll start to burn. You might even feel little wet blisters forming, filling with pus, then erupting as the smallest imperfection glides over them like a rolling pin. Pus will seep down into the socket, inside the wounds, and cause an infection in the blood. The patient might think she's getting sick, just a little head cold, not a big deal, though she hates having to deal with it when her new eye is bugging her, and she really doesn't want to make a big fuss about it—after all, she is not a victim—but it gets worse, and fast. A fever starts to burn her up. Doesn't even start low-grade, just hits her like a shotgun blast. She can't eat. She feels dizzy. Her skin burns, and she can't seem to keep her thoughts straight. She may even fall. Everything goes shiny, and the infection clogs a blood vessel until the pressure becomes too much and she hemorrhages. She has a stroke, and even if she doesn't die, she won't be able to talk. She won't be able to feed herself. She won't be able to recognize her kids or even herself anymore. She'll be just a brown paper bag, all because I didn't take enough time with the mold.

That's why I should've been paying more attention when I poured the alginate into Mr. Montgomery's left eye socket. He'd been in a bar fight that had gone south. It happened at Cousin's, this smoky dive off 65th and May. Said he'd just been minding his own business, smoking his third straight Camel while slamming his fourth straight Tito's and tonic, when this drunk guy started talking to him, asked him for his lighter. Mr. Montgomery handed it to him, but then the drunk guy pocketed it. Lit his smoke, puffed on it, then placed Mr. Montgomery's gray Bic into his jacket pocket. When Mr. Montgomery said something about it, that's when the man grabbed a Budweiser beer bottle and slammed it into Mr. Montgomery's eye. The glass shattered, and the brown glass eviscerated his eyeball. Doctors tried to save it but couldn't, and he ended up with an enucleation and an appointment in my office a few weeks later to get fitted for a custom prosthetic.

But my mind was elsewhere. While I had his head leaned back and a plastic syringe inserted into his socket, pouring the alginate to form the mold, I was thinking about my banker. He was a nice enough guy. Young, hair slicked back with product, suit pants a little too tight for him. But he was wondering why I was past due on my interest payment, why I was maxed out and hadn't been revolving the balance, just wanting to check in to make sure everything was all right. Smug little shit. Of course everything wasn't all right.

And that's when I made a mistake. I didn't let the alginate sit long enough. I was distracted. I pulled it from the socket, and my finger distorted the mold. It was just a slight imperfection, and I should've started over, cleared my head, taken my time, and done it again. But I didn't because sometimes the cost of things seems so much greater in the present than in the future.

◢▼◣

Growing up, I never really thought about what I wanted to be. Not sure the reason why. Some kids want to be a firefighter and others a detective, but the thought of what I wanted to be at some ephemeral date in the future, a length of time I was incapable of fathoming at that time of my life, just seemed unimportant. Besides, there was just so much going on when I was growing up. It was the early nineties, and I lived with my grandfather, Curt. He was the only family I had left. Both my parents were gone. They'd died in a car accident one night, my father too drunk to keep the car from swerving off Benedict Bridge into Sandstone Creek at more than fifty miles an hour. My grandmother had taken off to North Dakota with some guy who worked in the oil fields, so it was Grandpa Curt that was stuck with me.

Grandpa Curt and I lived in his old Pontiac. Basically, anyways. He had a house in Ponca City, but we were hardly ever there, and spent most of our time traveling around Tulsa and Bartlesville and Wichita and Joplin. He was a salesman, hocking surgical supplies to hospitals all around Oklahoma, Kansas, Arkansas, and Missouri, and because he had no one to look after me, I tagged along. It wasn't a bad way to grow up. I got used to the roadside travel stops, living off of Gatorades and Cheetos, washing my hair in public-restroom sinks, drying it underneath the hand dryers strapped to the walls. The only thing I brought with me on these trips was a small kaleidoscope. It was gold colored, long, and heavy, and it had belonged to my mother. It was the last thing of hers I had, really, and when I looked through it, I saw these brilliant greens and purples and blues and yellows mingling together to form geometric designs like snowflakes, and each time I felt afraid or lonely or sad, I could look through that glass and feel like I was with my mother again, curled up at our old home, warm and safe. That's why my grandfather called me his mosaic girl—I perceived the world through a fragmented lens.

One day, we were in Fayetteville visiting the surgical wing. My grandfather had an appointment with a Dr. Fairchild, an orthopedic surgeon. He was an older guy, late fifties, hair the color of dirty cotton and a noticeable burn scar on his neck. Sometimes during the sales calls, the doctors would allow me to scrub in and visit the operating room prior to the surgery commencing, and they'd show me the different instruments they used, the scalpels and anesthesia. At first, it was sort of interesting, knowing that in just a little while, a patient would be wheeled in, put under, and sliced open, but eventually the newness wore off, and it, like most everything else in this world if given enough time, turned banal.

This time was a little different, though. Usually, there would be nurses in there prepping for the surgery, ensuring the instruments were sterile and that the doctor had everything he needed, but this time the OR was empty. It was just me, Grandpa Curt, and Dr. Fairchild, and they were discussing a new eye speculum, but Grandpa Curt couldn't seem to find it in his bag.

"I'm so sorry," he said. "I must've left it in my car." He then turned to me and said, "You okay by yourself?"

Eleven years old and not wanting to look like a child in front of the doctor, I told him sure, and Grandpa Curt turned to leave.

It was just the doctor and me then. He was a tall man, taller than Grandpa Curt, and he smelled like most doctors I'd met, of soap and exhaustion.

"You know what this is?" he asked. He picked up a bone saw.

I shook my head no even though I knew exactly what it was. I might have been only eleven, but I knew when best not to answer a man honestly.

"The patient that's about to come in here is diabetic. Foot and ankle are covered in ulcers. You know what ulcers are?"

"No."

"They're these deep sores where the skin has fallen off and the underlying tissue is exposed. Oftentimes, they get dirty, and they get infected, and eventually, if other treatments don't work, I have to use this saw here and—" He picked up the bone saw and turned it on. The blade whizzed around so fast it hummed. "You want to hold it?"

"I'm sorry?"

The doctor's eyes went wide and he had this look like he was offering me a cookie. "Do you want to hold it?"

I didn't want to. I just wanted Grandpa Curt to return, to finish up this sales call so we could get back in the car and make it to the next hospital on our list, but it was a long way to the parking lot, and Grandpa Curt didn't move all that fast anymore.

"I probably shouldn't. Aren't you about to use it?"

"You washed your hands well, didn't you? And you've got gloves on."

I hesitated, trying to think of a way to stall.

"Come on," he said. "It'll be fun."

I approached, and Dr. Fairchild held up the bone saw. It looked a bit like Grandpa Curt's handheld electrical drill, with a long black handle supporting a cylindrical top encased in black plastic. The blade extended out from this. It was long, rectangular, and flat, shaped not unlike a giant stick of gum, the edges sharp and glistening under the fluorescent light.

"Take it here," the doctor said, holding it up to me. "Be careful of the trigger. Don't press it until you absolutely mean to."

I wrapped my hand around the handle, and the doctor slipped his hand over mine. His fingers ran down my fingers; I knew what he was doing. He scooted in close to me and positioned his face next to my ear, so that I could feel his wet breath against my cheek.

"It's exciting, isn't it?" he asked, and I wanted to pull the trigger and push the blade right into his belly. "Do you like it?" He pressed his body up against mine, and I could feel him through his pants. It was the first time, but not the last, a man pressed up against me without me wanting him to. I was too young then to say "no," to rebuke him and pull away. I just stood there frozen, unsure what I should do, but before the doctor could do anything else, Grandpa Curt returned.

"Sorry about that," he said. "Left it in my trunk like an idiot."

After the sales call, I sat up front with Grandpa Curt, him warming his hands over the heater vents, and me trying to find the courage to tell him what had happened. But I couldn't. The words just fizzled out on my tongue. Too worried he wouldn't believe me or, worse yet, blame me for the doctor's advances, I said nothing.

"Something wrong?" he asked.

"No, Grandpa."

I could still feel his eyes on me, his worried expression reflected in the window pane.

"I know what you need," he said. He turned to the backseat and grabbed my kaleidoscope.

I took it from him but didn't look through it. The world was crooked without me making it more so. Instead, I stared out at the dense, gray fog on the horizon, the weight of the kaleidoscope no longer as heavy in my hand.

"My mosaic girl," he said. "Things will turn around soon."

◢▼◣

Marcie wouldn't sleep by herself. Not in her bed. Not in a sleeping bag on the floor next to mine. She'd only sleep if she was touching me. She wouldn't collapse until well after midnight, her tiny body snuggled up against mine, her arms and legs continuously punching and kicking me in my face and ribs. My pediatrician had told me to avoid co-sleeping, said it might warp my daughter's development, but I was too tired to fight her anymore. Every night it was the same thing. First, a dinner of frozen chicken nuggets or Hamburger Helper, something quick but hot that tasted a tad bit better than pencil shavings, the entire time Marcie pushing away her plate and tossing the food on the floor. Then a bath. Marcie would play with her cars, splashing water all over the tile floor, just another thing I'd have to clean up, and she'd fight me as I washed her body and her hair, the no-tear formula causing a whole mess of tears regardless of the bottle's promises. Once dry, she'd chew on her toothbrush instead of actually brushing her teeth, spitting the blue goo all over the counter instead of in the sink. I'd read her a book afterward, *Fancy Nancy*, *Knock Knock*, or something by Dr. Seuss, and I'd tuck her in. I'd kiss her on the forehead and plead with her to please, just please stay in your bed tonight. Nothing bad will happen. I promise. Mommy's just in the other room. But it never worked.

That night, just like all the rest of the nights, Marcie slung open the door to the master, strolled in with her pajamaed feet kicking high, her arms swinging around her like she was the one who paid the mortgage. She smacked her lips and made this popping sound and strolled up right next to my bed.

"Momma," she said. I feigned being asleep, hoping she might give up and return to her bed. "Momma? Momma?" She tapped her little hand on the back of my head, trying to get my attention, but still I pretended to be asleep. "Momma, phone. Phone. Momma, phone."

I could hear her grabbing my phone from the nightstand. She spent most of her time on it, watching YouTube videos and playing this putt-putt game, sort of. Mostly she just shot the ball around, clanging it against obstacles and up ramps without regard to actually getting the ball in the hole, but she was enamored with the lights and the game and the noises it made. I hated the fact she spent so much time glued to a screen, but it was the only time I had to myself, where she wasn't climbing on me, tugging at my pant leg, demanding my energy, my love, my complete and utter attention at all times, and so I let her play on it. But not that night. I was determined. I got up, I took her hand, and I told her no.

"It is time to go night-night."

I grabbed her by the hand and led her out of the room. She immediately threw a fit, crumpling to the floor, her free hand balled up into a fist, trying to wiggle out from my grip.

"No, ma'am," I told her. "That's not how we act. You're a big girl now. It's time for you to start sleeping in your own bed."

I dragged her over the carpet as she kicked and screamed and cried, but eventually we made it to her door. I had to grab ahold of her to keep her from struggling, pinning her arms against her sides. Her face was the color of red velvet cake, and a worm of snot snaked its way down to her upper lip.

"Please, baby. Mommy is tired. Will you please sleep in your room?"

"No!" She spat when she yelled this, all over my face.

I breathed in. I held it for a moment. Counted backward from ten. "Baby, please. I know you're too young to understand, but I'm just so exhausted. I need a little sleep. Please."

I tried laying her in her bed, tucking her under the covers, but she continued to scream. She threw the blankets off of her, sat up in bed, and tried to wiggle past me. Three years old, she was big for her age, but I recalled the pediatrician's warnings and fretted that she wasn't developing properly. She had no interest in potty training; every time we tried, she would just play with her little plastic toilet, putting it over her head while naked, her smooth little butt wiggling back and forth as she danced. Even more worrisome, her vocabulary wasn't where it should have been. She could speak, and I understood her, or at least some of what she said, her words smooshed, her tongue pressed against the roof of her mouth as she said "phone" or "Mario," but there was such a stark contrast when I took her on playdates with kids her own age, how crystalline their words were, how they were beginning to speak in full sentences, and deep down inside I felt shame and embarrassment and like a failure as a mother, and this would transform into a seething rage toward Marcie. I hated this, I did, but I couldn't help it. It burned inside of me.

"Stop it," I said. "No. You have to sleep in here."

I grabbed her by the arms, but she wriggled free, screamed, and balled up her little fist before hitting me in the eye. The world fragmented, visions of broken beer bottles and bone saws coalesced into a kaleidoscopic mirage, and I lost it. I shook her. I screamed at her. I smacked her across the face, harder than I meant to. Her cheek turned pink, and she stopped crying for a moment, her eyes wide in desperation and shock and fear, and I only wanted to disappear. Grab my bag and leave and drive until I ran out of gas. It didn't even matter which direction, just as far away from her as I could possibly get, but I knew this to be a fantasy. I was trapped.

"I'm so sorry, sweet girl," I said instead, hugging her, caressing her back and telling her I loved her, and I led her back to my bed, where she curled up beside me, her little hand caressing my chin, her tiny foot digging into my gut, keeping me from sleep.

◢▼◣

It just didn't make sense. I refreshed the webpage to my company's bank account, but still it said $2.30. There should have been a deposit of roughly $30,000 that morning, payments owed to me by private insurance companies for eyes I'd fitted for patients, but it wasn't there. I refreshed again, and again it said only $2.30. I picked up the phone and called my medical billing vendor, Claim Logic.

"Thank you for calling Claim Logic, this is Bethany. How may I help you?"

"Yes, hi. This is Cooper Cloud with Prosthetic Eye Tech. Was wondering if you could let me know if my reimbursement has been delayed?"

I could hear her typing away on her computer, and after a few questions to verify my identity, she went silent.

"Hello? Did I lose you?"

She made some weird noises, a mixture of "ums" and gargles, like she couldn't decide whether to answer or clear her throat.

"One moment, Ms. Cloud."

"Wait, wait, wait. I just—" But she didn't wait. I was accosted by their soft-jazz hold music. I put the phone on speaker and refreshed the webpage to my online banking. Still no deposit. Still only $2.30. Still had to make payroll in two days. Both my office manager, Janice, and assistant, Cheri, needed to get paid, plus my rent, materials, utilities, insurance, mortgage, food, phone, daycare, and on and on and on. I was past due on a few items: my company's insurance and a bill for five hundred stock eyeballs that were sitting in the back of my car. I had their past-due notices next to the computer, the first bills I was going to pay that morning. I refreshed again, smashing my finger on the enter button. New balance, -$2,489.72, the numbers jumping through the screen in a resplendent red.

The soft jazz stopped. A new voice was on the other end, a man this time. "Mrs. Cloud, I apologize for the wait. This is Jerome Maldonado. Your reimbursement was not delayed. Payment was received and remitted to your bank."

"I do not see it in my bank account. Usually there like clockwork. Fifth of every month, I get my deposit. Been that way for two years now. But it's not there."

"You should call your bank."

"I'm calling you. Where is my money?"

"Ma'am, you really should call your bank."

I picked up the receiver and slammed it back down, and that's when I noticed it. My line of credit balance was down $28,000. It had been fully advanced and now it wasn't. The bank had taken my money and didn't even ask me. Fine. Whatever. I'd just make an advance and deposit the balance. I clicked on the transfer button, told it to move $28,000 from my line to my operating account, hit enter, but it didn't work. I tried again, and again it didn't work. I tried a third time, but the money wouldn't move. Each time, I got an error message telling me "Oops, something went wrong. If this continues, please give us a call."

Fuck give us a call. I was going down there.

The bank was only a mile down from my office on the other side of the highway, the main reason I chose it when I'd started out a couple of years back. It was a small building, orange bricked, gable roofed, a clock tower rising into the sky. Inside, it was all dark wood and cream-colored tile, replete with smartly dressed and beautiful young people. Back in the corner office was my banker. He had a customer with him, some old guy wearing a plaid shirt too tight for him, tucked into some Wranglers.

"What the fuck did you do with my money, Josh?"

He pushed himself back from the desk when I barged in, hands raised as if to protect himself. His customer just smiled up at me with this smug-ass grin, like I amused him.

"This isn't the time, Cooper. You need to set an appointment."

"My kid might starve, Josh. My appointment is now." I turned to the old man. "Get out." He didn't move, though. He looked instead like he wished he had a bag of popcorn. "Get. The Fuck. Out." I smacked him across the shoulder once, twice, three times, and finally he got up and left. Josh stood like he might do something, but he was a coward. He just stood there like he didn't know what to do with his hands.

"I'm going to call security," he said.

"You took my money."

"You defaulted on your loan, Cooper. Your insurance lapsed. Hell, we got notice this morning you're being sued for malpractice by a James Montgomery. Until you pay us back in full, we're going to lock-box your receivables."

The lawsuit was news to me, and it hit me right in the gut. I could feel the lining in my stomach simmer. I hadn't paid my malpractice insurance. If he won—and remembering that too-soft alginate, I knew he would—I'd be ruined. I'd have my license revoked. I wouldn't be able to practice again until I paid him in full, and he could win hundreds of thousands of dollars. I needed that deposit.

"Lockbox my receivables? What does that mean?"

"You need to calm yourself, Cooper, or I'm going to have to call security."

"What in the hell does that mean, Josh?"

"It means you won't be paid until we're paid back in full."

The sheer magnitude of it all squashed me. I owed the bank over $200,000. It would take nine months before I could pay them back. Nine months before I could pay my employees or my vendors or buy groceries or pay my mortgage. Nine months before I could pay my attorney to defend me. I wouldn't be able to do it. All my savings had been used to start my business. Everything I had, had been poured into my work, into this dream, this stupid fantasy I had that I could make Marcie's and my life better. Now it had hardened into dusty coal, choking me from the inside out.

"You're bankrupting me, Josh," I said.

"I'm sorry, Cooper, but you've bankrupted yourself."

With nothing else to say, I left. The tellers and customers all stared at me out of their peripherals, fully aware of the scene I had just caused, but not wanting to make eye contact lest I did something desperate. A security guard followed me until I was outside. I unlocked my car, started the ignition, and turned to reverse out of my parking spot. In the backseat were the two boxes of eyeballs I hadn't, and wouldn't, be able to pay for. Couldn't return them, either. They were just useless glass marbles now. Collateral for the bank. That was their only utility. I supposed I could donate them, but the bank would probably sue me for that, too. Well, if Josh insisted on collateral, then Josh could have them. I picked up a box and carried it back inside. Josh stood there along with the security guard, the tellers behind them hiding behind their computers, their young, pretty faces contorted into a mixture of fear and amusement.

"Don't do anything stupid," Josh said.

"I believe these are yours," I said. "Consider it a down payment." I turned the box upside down and dumped hundreds of eyeballs onto the lobby floor, spreading and bouncing like the shattered contours of my kaleidoscopic dream.

◢▼◣

Back home I tried to stick to my routine, to not let Marcie see me break down. We ate dinner at the table: boxed macaroni and cheese and the last of our Dr. Pepper. She, of course, didn't eat much, instead flinging the yellow noodles all over the floor and herself. She spilled her glass, dumping the contents all over my plate, but I was too tired and scared to rebuke her. Soon, our pantry would be empty, the bank would foreclose on the house, and she'd go hungry and cold and be scared and confused, and although I would tell her that everything would be okay, that Mommy just needed some time to figure stuff out, to find a job, to pay her debts, she wouldn't understand. She'd believe me at first, but if I couldn't find a job, if I couldn't sell the house, if we had to move into our car, staying mobile so the bank couldn't find us and take that, too, she'd stop believing. She'd lose her trust in me, and slowly she'd grow to resent me, until all she had to look forward to was uncertainty and thirst.

After dinner, I gave her a bath. She demanded bubbles and played with toy cars in the water, crashing them into one another while making collision noises and splashing water and bubbles all over the bath mat. I didn't try to stop her, though. I was too tired to fight with her. Besides, she needed to be a kid for as long as she could, to take comfort in warm water and lavender-scented soap. Before too long, she might forget what this moment was like, when she'd felt safe and loved. I let her play a little longer than normal, waiting until the bathwater turned cool and she began to shiver. For once, she didn't complain when I began to drain the water. She just reached up with her little crab hands, saying, "Cold, Momma. Cold." I dried her off and wrapped the towel around her body and didn't complain when she chewed on her toothbrush, or when she missed the sink spitting out her toothpaste. And when she screamed and cried when we tried to put on her pajamas, I didn't force them on her. If she wanted to go without, then she would go without.

"Marcie, darling. I need to tell you something."

"Choo choo, Momma. Choo choo." She wanted to play a game on my phone. A game where a train outran obstacles trying to derail it off its course. She loved it, though she wasn't very good at it, her only strategy to barrel ahead at full speed regardless of what stood in her way.

"Things are going to get tough around here for a while. You're going to have to be a big girl for me. Do you understand?"

"Phone, Momma. Choo choo."

"You're going to have to learn not to rely on me always being there. You understand?"

"Choo choo."

In the kitchen, I found a screwdriver, unscrewed the bathroom doorknob, put it on her bedroom door, and placed her inside. I then locked the door from the outside. She screamed at the top of her lungs, "Mommy, Mommy, please, Mommy," and I told her not to worry. One day she'd be brave like me, a mosaicked woman, making choices a bit crooked.

Ghost Stories

NOAH MILLIGAN

My brother, before he died,
had told stories about our childhood home,
claiming it to have been haunted.

I remember the stories, too,
like the one when we'd been awakened
by dishes flung across the kitchen
although no one was there to throw them.

My brother and I witnessed this alone
while standing in the hallway,
socked feet rubbing against carpet,
fueled by static electricity.

We often recount these stories now,
my father, mother, and I
when gathered around the kitchen table,
eating pecan pie laced with nostalgia.

But memory is a funny thing,
fluid and unreliable.
I'm more convinced it's easier
to blame ghosts than the living.

Ghosted

K. Y. ROBINSON

HE FIRST TIME CYNTHIA SAW TROY, SHE could feel flowers sprouting inside her ribcage. He was sitting at the table next to hers in a quaint midtown-Houston coffee shop enclosed by lush greenery, and each time he lowered his newspaper, she stole glimpses of his cinnamon-brown eyes and red-clay skin bathed by the sunlight streaming through the window. Even the sun wants to kiss him, she thought to herself.

"Take a picture. It'll last longer." Troy slapped his paper down on the table but regarded her with a crooked smile, revealing dimples she wanted to sink into.

"It's funny you should say that. I'm a photographer," Cynthia said with a confidence she didn't feel, pulling a camera from her canvas backpack.

"No, you are a garden, full of beauty I want to drink in." His eyes consumed her. She gave herself to his hunger.

For the next hour, they talked about their careers, hobbies, and life in the Bayou City. Troy was well-travelled and charming. His childhood consisted of Jack & Jill parties and summering in Oak Bluff while Cynthia had spent her formative years scratching and surviving inner-city poverty and violence. Although they were from different worlds, the chemistry between them was undeniable.

The next eight months were all late-night calls, hungry kisses, and sweating bodies. She, his garden he'd play in; he, her everything. Troy, a workaholic corporate lawyer, issued strings of broken promises. Cynthia, an insecure but fulfilled art teacher, nagged him more than she wanted. Troy teased her about wanting nothing more than to own a studio and gallery and become a full-time photographer.

Usually all smiles when she picked him up from the airport, this time Troy's mouth didn't soften when he saw her at the baggage carousel. The fire that had burned in his eyes was extinguished. An ocean divided them though they were only inches apart. She hoped he would ask her to stay when she pulled into his driveway, but the invite never came. He thanked her for the ride and quickly grabbed his luggage from the trunk. He didn't kiss her goodbye. Maybe he was jet-lagged and needed some rest, she thought.

Over the next few days, her text messages and calls went unanswered. She made up more excuses: Maybe he was really busy at work. Maybe he had a lot on his mind. She showed up at the coffee shop, hoping to run into him. She went to his Facebook page searching for clues that justified his absence but realized he had unfriended her. Her feelings fluctuated between confusion, disbelief, and despair. What had she done to deserve this? Why was he so intent on disconnecting from her? Didn't the last eight months mean anything?

The loss consumed her. The breakup began to feel like a breakdown. Food was unpalatable and sleep eluded her. She couldn't accept that it was over without an explanation. She kept rewinding and replaying everything that had happened between them like a video, searching for the moment their relationship changed course. Every morning, she put his navy blazer from the coatrack to her nose and inhaled remnants of tobacco and cologne. It was the only tangible thing left of him. The ghosts of what they once were resided in every corner of her loft: Phantom kisses on her forehead. The specter of him working on his laptop at the kitchen table, looking up every so often to smile at her, dimples deepening. The spirits of them swaying to Nina Simone's "Wild Is the Wind" underneath the warm glow of string lights in the community garden. As days turned into weeks, her hopes of reconciliation, of contact—of anything—diminished. The writing was on the wall no matter how much she wanted to smear it and write in her own fairytale instead.

Jazmine suggested she try online dating to distract herself and move on, but the thought of it filled her with anxiety. If she was this unlucky when it came to love in the real world, how could she fare any better online? Cynthia examined the profile Jazmine built for her, trying to work up the nerve to press the submit button. All she saw was an exaggerated version of herself, her skin-tight dress accentuating curves she usually concealed, her hair straightened, and her lips painted ruby red. Although the sexy makeover had been fun and a much-needed ego boost, she wondered if she could live up to the fantasy of the glossed-up pics when she felt a plain Jane at heart. As her mind began to drift further down Brokenhearted Lane, Jazmine arrived at her door.

"You still haven't finished it yet?" Jazmine said, reaching for the wireless mouse on the desk, nearly spilling Cynthia's cup of coffee.

"I don't think online dating is for me. What ever happened to meeting people the organic way?"

"Girl, you need to get with the program. It's cuffing season," Jazmine said, unwrapping her breakfast sandwich and taking a meticulous bite, careful not to smear her freshly painted lips.

"People can pretend to be anyone online. I mean, look at my profile pic! What if I end up meeting a serial killer?"

"First of all, everyone glams up their profile. Second, and more importantly, I think you're just making excuses because you think Troy is coming back," Jazmine said, rolling her eyes. "I know you still have feelings for him, but he ghosted you almost a month ago! Don't you think it is time to move on?"

Cynthia looked away as tears welled up in her eyes. Her best friend of fifteen years could read her like a book. She was always there to lend an ear and offer a shoulder to cry on, but Jazmine also reeled her back into reality whenever she drifted too far from it. She had her best interests at heart with her tough love and no-nonsense advice. Jazmine was right. She was leaving the door open for Troy, and maybe it was time to shut it for good. His sudden disappearance told her all she needed to know about their so-called connection. There wasn't any, at least not anymore. She hovered the mouse pointer over the icon and submitted her profile as Jazmine shimmied in solidarity. Cynthia shook her head and laughed in spite of herself.

Over the next few days, Cynthia's inbox was flooded with messages. They were both overwhelming and underwhelming. Overwhelming due to the quantity of men who responded, underwhelming due to the quality of those responses. It was all the same sexual innuendo, the same phone number requests from guys who were too lazy to complete their profiles. It was as if they were all using cookie-cutter responses. Cynthia, who loathed pointless small talk with strangers, who avoided people and favored her vinyls and cozy apartment, forced herself to listen to Jazmine's voice in her head about getting with the times. The thought often crossed her mind that Troy might find out that she was dating. Maybe he'd see her in that red dress and realize he missed her. Maybe his message would be next in her inbox. *I missed you, my garden, my darling. Please take me back.*

She shook her head, chastising herself. I will go out with the next person that sends a message. The very next person, she thought. A few seconds later, a message from Derek, a field supervisor at a petroleum plant, popped up on her screen. They made plans to meet at a bistro on his lunch break the very next day. Cynthia was the first to arrive and had her back to the door when he entered. He called out her name loudly, and fellow patrons turned their heads to see who he was talking to. Cynthia felt like disappearing. After lifting her hand in a small wave, she instantly regretted it. This man didn't know the concept of an inside voice and looked significantly older than his profile pic. Cynthia was far from vain, but he had outright lied. After he complimented her feet a few times too many for comfort, she excused herself to the restroom and snuck out through a fire exit.

Her next date was with Russel, a correctional officer with piercing blue eyes, a Greek god in a cowboy hat. They met at a Mexican restaurant for Taco Tuesday. He downed several shots of tequila, tried to pet Cynthia's afro, and told her that he'd "never experienced a chocolate woman before." When she rejected his distasteful advances, he called her every racial epithet he could think of before driving away in a pickup truck displaying stickers of Calvin from "Calvin & Hobbes" peeing on something. Russel was later dubbed Bigot Brad when this tirade went viral on social media. Instead of coming to Cynthia's aid during the event, people just pressed record on their cell phones. On the walk home, Cynthia vowed off technology, online dating, social media, all of it. Somehow it had changed what it meant to be human. To have empathy. That handheld brick made it possible for people to simply disengage themselves whenever it suited them.

A couple of weeks and several nudges from Jazmine went by before Cynthia logged in to check her messages. She was so discouraged. If dating online was the new wave, why did it feel like she was drowning? She gave it one more chance, repeating to herself as she logged in, "The third time's a charm." She narrowed down the parameters of what she was looking for even though it would limit her options. She was matched with three men. The first one was Brian, a thirty-something sociologist. His hobbies and interests included writing, working out, museums, live music, community service, and political activism. His profile impressed her. He almost seemed too good to be true. As she scrolled through his photo album, one photo took her by surprise. It was Brian in a group photo with his frat brothers, one of whom was Troy. Her heart all but stopped. An ache engulfed her. She stared at Troy, his dimple flashing. As her finger poised to swipe left, she felt a sudden sadness. How on earth could she date Troy's friend?

Hello Cynthia. Thanks for checking out my profile. I see that you're a teacher. Since I was a kid, I've been a people watcher. It was only natural for me to become a sociologist. What about you?

It wasn't like Cynthia was going into this with the plan of hurting Brian. After all, he did seem like a nice guy. She just wanted closure on that time of her life. Then she could truly move on. This was her way of finding Troy to do that—through Brian. She promised herself she'd meet with Troy just once to find out why he had changed his mind.

Hi Brian. I really liked your profile. To answer your question, I've always turned to art to escape and understand the world, so I wanted to teach others how to channel their creativity, too.

When she told Jazmine what had happened over mimosas and frittatas, Jazmine frowned and shook her head in confusion. "So, you're going to mess up what you could have with the new guy to see why things went wrong with the old guy?"

"I'm not going to mess up anything! You don't know what it's like to have someone leave and never tell you why," Cynthia said, offended by Jazmine's snap judgment.

"If you need to find out what happened, I understand, but don't drag an innocent man into this. It ain't right," Jazmine said, placing money on the table for her half of the tab. "Damn it, Cynthia, you break your own heart more than anyone else ever could."

After chatting for over a week, Brian and Cynthia went on their first date, to a museum for an exhibition and short film. During a candlelit dinner, she waited for the moment the date would end in disaster. She expected a secret wife to storm their table and throw a drink in his face, for him to admit he had five kids by five women, for him to say he just wasn't that interested. Nothing like that happened. She didn't want him to jump into her bed, and the evening felt comfortable and soft. It was so comfortable, she felt she could approach the subject of his friends without seeming like she was fishing for information.

"So, I saw that you're a member of Kappa Alpha Psi. Do you still keep in touch with your frat brothers?" Cynthia asked nonchalantly, taking a bite of her dessert.

"Yes, I am. I pledged when I was a junior at Morehouse. I'm still in contact with a few of them."

"Okay . . . cool. Do any of them live here in town?"

Before he could answer the question, his phone rang. Worry

swept across his face. He had a family emergency and needed to cut the date short. Cynthia briefly wondered if it was a ruse to leave the date early without looking like a jerk, but he was apologetic as he paid the bill and promised to make it up to her.

Over the next week, Brian kept in constant contact with Cynthia while he was out of town tending to his ailing grandmother, who had broken a hip. She found it endearing because she'd barely ever heard from Troy when he was out of town. When Brian returned, he invited Cynthia over to his place to make her his "famous lasagna." She saw this as a perfect way to take her investigation to another level, searching for pictures of his friends—and Troy.

After catching up over wine and chopping vegetables, he shooed her from the kitchen to keep his treasured recipe a secret. He handed her the remote and told her to make herself at home.

As she made her way around the living area, the pictures that adorned his rustic fireplace told the story about Brian's heritage and life: his enslaved great-great-grandfather, relics from the civil rights era, and assorted family photographs. Cynthia was in awe of Brian's extensive knowledge of his roots; she always felt so disconnected from hers.

"This is impressive," Cynthia called to him, slowly tracing her finger along the mantel. "I couldn't even tell you who my ancestors were."

"Thank you." Brian poked his head out of the kitchen, taken aback by the compliment. "If you don't know your history, you're bound to repeat it. If you'd like, I can help you with your research."

"Really? You would do that? That would be great," Cynthia said. "Hmm, it's smelling good in there."

"You can come back in now. Here, try this. I guarantee it's the best meat sauce you'll ever taste." Brian walked over to her, stood close, and held the wooden spoon against Cynthia's awaiting mouth as she took a careful sip.

"Wow," she said. "I think you're right. It's really good." They lost themselves in each other's eyes for a moment.

"Good enough to kiss the cook?"

Cynthia caught herself. "Maybe." She turned away abruptly, making her way back to the living area. She didn't want to kiss him, especially this soon. She was there on a mission, not to end up in a missionary position!

The weather was pleasantly cool and mild, so they decided to have dinner on the patio overlooking the lake. Cynthia busied herself with eating and nursing her glass of wine to compensate for the silence. She wondered if she had hurt Brian's feelings by not kissing him.

"About earlier," Brian said, breaking the awkwardness. "I'm sorry. I was caught up in the moment."

"It's okay," Cynthia said, touching his hand. "It just surprised me, that's all." Once the awkwardness dissipated, dinner became filled with so much ease and laughter, she forgot about snooping.

After spending more time together over the next few weeks, Cynthia's feelings for Brian shifted from platonic to romantic. His bronze, chiseled face exuded patience and kindness. She noticed how charming he looked when his glasses would slip to the end of his nose whenever he was in deep concentration, and he would absentmindedly push them back up. His warm smile had the potential to melt the glaciers. His soft, dark eyes looked at her like she was the only woman in the world. The chemistry between Cynthia and Brian was a slow, sweet burn. She realized it had been unwise to rely on instant fireworks to determine compatibility. Fireworks fizzled in the end, after all—just like they had with Troy.

She began fantasizing about Brian. She yearned to become a garden again. To be tended by his strong and attentive hands. To be watered by his kisses and bloom furiously. One night she showed up at his front door unannounced—a bold move on her part. They gazed at each other for a long moment with an overwhelming longing they could no longer deny.

"Are you sure about this?" Brian asked, cupping Cynthia's face and slowly inching his lips toward hers. "Because there's no turning back after you've kissed the cook."

"Yes," she said breathlessly, undoing the buttons of his shirt. "I'm so tired of looking back."

The more Cynthia and Brian were tangled in the vines of desire over the next few months, the less she thought about Troy. She lost sight of her original plan. One morning, she stopped reaching for his blazer and reached for a box instead. As she donated the jacket, she felt free. She stopped walking down Brokenhearted Lane. She realized memory is a funny thing, fluid and unreliable. The memories no longer sustained her. Jazmine was right: she had broken her own heart more than Troy ever had. The present was waiting for her to arrive.

After a litany of failed relationships, Brian was the soft landing she'd been searching for, and it was reassuring that the feeling was mutual. Though also an extrovert, Brian was different than Troy. He was warm and affable, approachable where Troy had been intimidating. Brian brought out a side of Cynthia that she never knew existed. He knew how to lure her out of her shell and help her take chances. With his encouragement, Cynthia took a leap of faith. She quit her job and rented out a space for a studio and gallery. Her quiet and introspective nature tamed his more impulsive tendencies and helped him see things from a different perspective. Through Cynthia, he learned unconventional ways to use sociology outside of a scientific framework and started working on a new book. The past several months had brought her a healing, a reconciliation with herself, and an illuminated path of what the future could hold for her. Having a support system in Jazmine also made the journey easier and it strengthened their friendship. When Jazmine began experiencing dating woes of her own, Cynthia returned the favor by being there for her and letting her vent to her heart's content.

With a glowing recommendation from her supportive beau, she was commissioned as a second photographer to cover his editor's destination wedding in the Cayman Islands. Her job entailed capturing candid moments and shooting different angles alongside the lead photographer, a well-known and sought-after artist. When she arrived on the idyllic island, it felt like a dream. The oceanfront villa overlooked the sparkling turquoise sea. The coconut palm trees, powder-white sand, and balmy sea breeze were a refreshing change from the humdrum of everyday city life. The happy couple exchanged their sacred vows of matrimony on the beach at sunset with the ocean as the backdrop. As she snapped shots, Cynthia found herself wishing Brian were there with her.

The reception was held inside the villa. As Cynthia took photos of the attendees on the dance floor, Troy appeared through the lens of her camera. When she zoomed in to confirm, it almost took her breath away. Six months, it had been. Six months of no explanation, no responses, nothing. And now, Troy was on this island a million miles away from their previous life, downing a rum cocktail with the groom. Don't see me, don't see me, don't see me, went through her head as she went outside to the balcony for fresh air and to collect her thoughts. Several deep breaths later and bolstered by the knowledge that she had to do her job, she headed back inside. Troy nearly walked straight into her as he was lighting his cigarette.

"Troy." She didn't know what else to say.

Troy dropped his cigarette, his look unreadable. A woman stepped onto the balcony and reached for his hand.

"Cynthia, this is my wife, Amber," Troy said, pulling out his linen handkerchief to wipe the beads of sweat sprouting on his forehead. He didn't know what type of reaction to expect. "Amber, this is Cynthia."

"Nice to meet you, Cynthia," Amber said sweetly as she placed her hand over her blooming belly. "Darling, I hope you're not out here smoking. You promised you would quit. It's bad for the baby." The back-to-back news about their marriage and the baby hit Cynthia like a ton of bricks and left her in a momentary daze. A few months ago, this news would've pushed her past her breaking point. Troy was the furthest thing from her mind when her long-burning questions were finally answered in a chance encounter. What were the odds of such a thing?

"Hello, Amber," Cynthia said, retrieving her video camera from its holster. "Congratulations. Do you two have a special message for Mr. & Mrs. Lancaster?"

Amber slipped her arm around her husband. "We wish you a very blissful marriage, Alex and Kevin!" As Amber continued giggling and offering her nuggets of wisdom for a lasting marriage as if she had been married a century, so much rushed through Cynthia. She'd thought if she ever saw Troy again it would break her. She'd thought she would be filled with rage. It was the opposite. The heavy backpack of heartbreak she had borne for so many months suddenly felt lighter. The resentment rolled away in gentle aquamarine waves. She realized the ghosts of her memories were lies. The phantom that kissed her on her forehead did so to avoid her lips. The specter glued to his laptop late at night was professing his undying devotion to Amber. The spirit that held her close only used her as a surrogate to quell his loneliness. While she'd been loving him, he was loving someone else.

Cynthia wasn't going to end Amber's world by telling her the truth—let her be his garden to play in. Her own world had ended for a brief moment in time, and she'd nearly lost herself. Him leaving was a blessing in disguise. If she hadn't broken free from the ghosts of what they once were, she wouldn't have found joy on the other side of the loss.

A few days later, Cynthia was sitting at her desk, going through the photos of the wedding. Brian entered the studio and kissed her on the cheek. "I figured you didn't have lunch yet, so I brought you something."

"Thank you," Cynthia said, eagerly taking a slice of pizza from the box.

"Are those pics from the wedding?"

"Yes, it was such a beautiful ceremony. I wished you were there, but I totally understand. How is Granny Bea, by the way?"

"She's recovering from her hip surgery in a rehab facility. They'll give her the care she needs until she can get around again on her own."

Cynthia nodded in agreement and kept scrolling through the photos until Brian abruptly stopped her. "Hey! That's my frat brother, Troy, and Amber! He finally married that woman," Brian exclaimed and let out a loud laugh.

"It's a small world," Cynthia said matter-of-factly, unsure how much she wanted to reveal.

Brian went on a spill about Troy and Amber's long-term relationship and how it had withstood the challenges and overcome the obstacles of infidelity, losing a child, and maintaining a long-distance relationship. Cynthia reflected on all this. It was a reminder that so much lies below what we cannot see.

Cynthia stood up out of her chair to face Brian and stared deeply into his eyes. She knew where love lived, and it was with him. There was more than heat between them. His love felt like rain after years of drought. He was the lighthouse leading her back home when she was wading in darkness. Her walls had softly tumbled down for him. He motivated her to make her dreams become a reality. He always made time for her, and she never had to exhume memories to keep her warm. What they shared was calm, soul-affirming, and grounding.

She placed her hand on his face and said, "True love stands the test of distance and time. I have a feeling that ours will, too."

"Yes it will, baby," he said, leaning in and giving her a kiss. "Yes it will."

Skin Hunger

K. Y. ROBINSON

loneliness, you say,
is a fluorescent fog
you can't see beyond
unless someone
is reaching for you
in the dark.
a hollow room echoing
in your ribcage
until someone
makes your bones sing.
a dark cloud
chasing you until
a sunlit mouth
breaks through
the overcast of your body.
i want to tell you that
their bodies
are not asylums,
windchimes,
or the only light
you'll ever carry but
sometimes i walk
down an aisle
in a grocery store
searching for a pair
of eyes to meet mine
to stop the hunger
from howling.

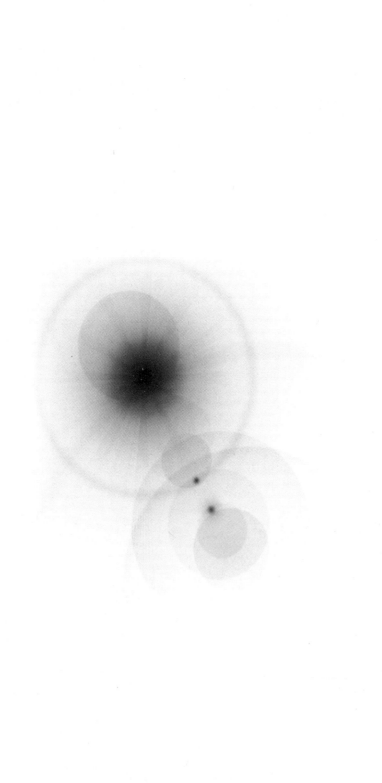

Halo

CAITLYN SIEHL

*W*HEN IT WAS TIME FOR MARGOT'S parents to change the season on her first birthday, they held her in their arms while they did it, and she watched their fingertips turn white and opaque, swirling like angry crystal balls as the clouds started to change, fall chasing away sticky summer heat. Margot lifted her own small hand, chubby and full of wonder, toward the sky, as if the only way to speak to it was to touch it.

She tried, every season for five years, to change the weather like her parents did. They stood on their balcony while the entire town and the news crews waited on the front lawn, hoping her fingers would light up and the storms would roll in. Nothing ever happened.

Margot had come into the world kicking, slightly underweight, and with a heart murmur. Small and frail and simple. No magic. No one knew why her eyes weren't cerulean, like her mother's, or emerald, like her father's, or why the sky gene wasn't passed down to her. No one knew what this would mean for the future. Eventually she stopped lifting her hands to the sky, choosing instead to stay behind with me while her parents did what they did every ninety-one and one-quarter days. When it was over, and the first flakes of snow were falling to the ground, I would catch them on my tongue while Margot ran in circles around the swing set.

Her mom blessed her with the water halo on her seventh birthday. Perhaps it was to prove that she was theirs, to prove that she was something worth protecting anyway. I remember her trying to see if she could trick her halo. In the pouring rain, she'd kick her feet into the mud like a raging bull, then race forward with her mouth clamped shut tightly. We thought she had almost outrun the halo once, but then the rain splashed, like it always did, on some invisible barrier above her head, bouncing off abruptly at a ninety-degree angle before landing on the ground about six inches away from her, leaving a perfect circle around her feet, her dress and skin dry.

I suppose I had always been in some kind of love with her, even when I was little and didn't know what it meant. She lived three houses down from me and chased fireflies on her front lawn with her friend Kiara. We spent every season change on Margot's lawn, Kiara's eyes toward the sky like everyone else's. Mine were on Margot.

"The fireflies like it when you sing to them," Margot called to me as she rounded the swing set. It was the time of summer when the cicadas were expected to unbury themselves from the ground. I was waiting for them.

"I'm not a good singer."

"It doesn't matter! They just like the noise. Here, I'll show you." She ran over to me and held my open palm, tracing a few of the small lines in it before she began to sing:

"How sad it is we'll never be, says the spider to the bee. She spins her web. He flies back home. How sad it is to be alone."

When I tore my eyes from her face, her brown skin turning golden in the sunset, there were no cicadas, but I had at least five lightning bugs sitting in my palm, their feelers wiggling all over my heart line. Kiara was standing right beside her, humming the song to herself.

"You have to name them before you let them go." Margot's eyes were fixed on one of the fireflies on her pointer finger. "They're more likely to come back if you do."

So I named them and followed both girls to a small maple tree, where I let them crawl away.

"I like your voice," I told Margot, positive I never wanted to stop hearing it.

The first time she kissed me, I thought the sky was falling and looked for her parents to see if they were watching from the bedroom window. We were eight and sharing a bubble-gum popsicle that we'd gotten from the ice-cream man. Margot often got free things because of her parents' control of the weather, and the ice-cream man needed good weather to do good business. We had licked through to the bubble-gum center, at which point began the fight for who got chewing rights.

"I'm older than you," she boasted, lips stained a bright, artificial pink.

"Yeah, by a month." Then we counted how many baby teeth we had left. Nine for me and seven for her, as it had been for the past six months. I watched, baffled, as she pulled the pink ball from the stick with her teeth. I pouted harder than usual, lips pushed out as I stared at the gum spilling out of her lips. She moved closer, until her knee was pressed against my knee: soft denim against soft denim.

"Wanna see the biggest bubble ever?"

I nodded, and she puffed up her chest and blew until a pink balloon the size of a grapefruit hung out of her mouth.

"Big whoop."

I crossed my arms over my chest but didn't look away. I never could.

She kneeled down right in front of me, so close I could see through the bubble and straight into her mouth, her teeth like popcorn kernels poking out of her gums.

"Gross!" I laughed and, just like that, she leaned in and kissed me until the bubble popped, only a thin film of goo separating our mouths. The sky turned dark for a brief moment, or I blinked. I was scared her parents had seen us and were angry enough to set dark clouds churning. Then she was gone, running, giggling, up the block back to her house, while I peeled the sticky gum off of my cheeks and chin, mumbling that we should just get two popsicles next time but knowing that we wouldn't.

That was the longest she ever kissed me. She had done it since, but she'd get fidgety and restless, and her leg would start bouncing like she wished she were moving. I remember pressing my ear to her sternum some nights while she was sleeping, happy to hear the normal, steady thrum of her heartbeat with the occasional double thump, like a glitch in a record player. Ba bump, ba bump, bump ba bump ba bump, ba bump. Watching her sleep was a strange experience. I would stay up a little later than her most nights just to look, half expecting her legs to kick out from under her, dog-dreaming. As impossible as it was for her to stay still during the day, at night her body was silent and poised and happy exactly where it was.

In my most selfish moments, I wished for that stillness during the day, for her to just sit beside me in the grass and stay in one place long enough for me to memorize the way the sun held the tight curls of her hair, or the way she looked when the thunder clapped.

As a teenager, nothing ever felt as good as touching Margot, as being touched by Margot. I loved her hands and her mouth and the way they knew exactly what to do and where to go. No fumbling in the dark, no shame. With Margot, I wanted to be something cataclysmic, like a dark cloud chasing her until my sunlit mouth broke through the overcast of her body. Something bright and inevitable, the way she was.

"That girl is like running water," Kiara said to me one night. We were seventeen and walking home from school together. Margot and I had just gotten into a fight because she didn't want to go to prom. She had run home before we could resolve it and left me with the familiar image of her body moving away from mine. Kiara stroked my hair on the way home, brushed the tears from my cheek with the soft pad of her thumb.

"I don't know if you'll be able to hold her for very much longer. You shouldn't beat yourself up about it. She'll go where she wants to go. She may be the freest soul out there, but she'll be lonelier for it."

"So will I," I said, repeating myself over and over again. I thought about her hair for the thousandth time, the backs of her knees, and what we'd look like dancing together in a place where people could see. "So will I. So will I. So will I."

I was eighteen when she and her parents left for California. She thought I hadn't seen the college brochures or the Berkeley sweatshirt under her bed, but I had. I kept quiet. I waited months for her to bring it up, to even mention the state at all, but it never happened, so we carried on as usual until I walked into her room and saw her reading over the welcome packet. It seemed strange that someone like her had to go to college at all. Princess of the Sky taking Earth Science,

I'd think to myself.

I wondered why her parents didn't just make her a throne in the sky instead, or send her to live in a castle in the middle of the Pacific Ocean until her powers had no choice but to kick in. California seemed mundane in comparison: Margot sleeping in a squeaky twin bed, sharing a room with some stranger who would try to remind her to bring an umbrella or to put on sunscreen.

"I'll be back once the plants get sick of my parents," she said the night I found out that they were leaving. I rolled over and traced her face with my index finger, trying to remember every detail of her nose and the way her eyelashes split into tiny white strands at the very tips. She turned her back to me after a while, careful to leave six inches of space between us because she knew I was going to start crying. She always knew.

In the end, she didn't love me anymore, and when you don't love someone anymore, the leaving is easier—sometimes even necessary. We spent the last of our days together packing up her house. I caught her with her fingers toward the sky a few times when she thought she was alone. I watched it remain undisturbed even as she looked at it with those eyes, not blue enough, not green enough, but some mixture that the clouds didn't understand.

"It's okay if you don't come back."

It was barely a whisper. She was moving too fast, as always, throwing three suitcases into their rented U-Haul while I held onto one of their lamps and watched from the sidewalk. Her hair was braided, I remember, thick black curls smooth and shiny, with two bright purple bands keeping them that way.

"I'm coming back," she said, voice emphatic and stubborn but not at all truthful.

We were silent when her parents came out and finished loading up, even more silent when her mom turned on the car and the rain, her way of saying goodbye because she knew her daughter wouldn't. Margot smiled, hands twitching at her sides the way they always did when her body wasn't moving. In every picture I had, some part of her was always blurry.

"I read that Berkeley has really nice dorm rooms . . ." I called after her as she ran back toward the house to get her backpack.

"I don't even have a roommate yet," was all she said before running inside.

Thunder started rumbling in the distance, and the sky turned gray. As she came back out, the winds whipped her yellow dress around her legs. She looked like a wheat field in the middle of a storm, braids swaying back and forth, trying to leave as she stood still, rooted in front of me for a brief and blissful second.

"Here's a box of stationery in case you find the time to write."

I had bought it four weeks prior—the day she started packing. The notepads had hummingbirds on them, and little pink flowers poking out of a branch that stretched across the bottom. She stared at the box a long time before her eyes came back to me, and for a moment, I saw pity there. The rain was coming down harder, and the wind had blown back my hood. The world was a hurricane, and Margot stood in the eye.

"I'll send you some pictures of the campus, okay?" She stuffed the stationery into the front pocket of her backpack, and then we turned to look at her house, the magnificent and vacant palace that we used to pretend was ours. The balcony where her parents started the seasons looked cold and ordinary without her on it. The pink of her two-story room was a dim glow, and I tried not to focus on it or remember that it was empty of us now. If I walked inside, it would echo like a place I didn't belong anymore.

"Have fun."

It wasn't the right thing to say, and I knew it when I turned back to look at her and she frowned, dark brows furrowing, her perfect mouth curving downward. Her mom honked the horn, her eyes looking at us through the rearview mirror, solemn and blue and powerful, the way the sky is.

"Don't forget to write."

I held her hand in mine, ran my thumb across the tightrope in her palm. She squeezed once, like it was a handshake, then let go.

We didn't kiss. Maybe it would all have been different if we had, if she'd planted her feet straight into the ground and stayed there long enough for me to taste the pink bubble gum of her mouth one last time. Maybe she would have remembered something important and stayed. Instead, she just smiled, her hair dry and shining while water soaked through my clothes and clung to my eyelashes. The wind whipped rain across my face and stuck her dress to her thighs. The yellow flowers stretched over the skin of her legs like tattoos.

"See you soon," she said, looking at me one last time before turning away. It was more of a goodbye than I'd ever gotten before, and I was struck still with it. I knew then, beyond anything, that I would never see her again, that she had packed up the last of our life together in her boxes and moved on, but I wanted to believe that she meant it.

She slammed the car door shut and they pulled away, the U-Haul rumbling behind them—a faithful dog full of memories. She didn't look back until they turned the corner at the end of the street, when her entire body turned to face me through the rain-streaked window, something unknowable and monumental in her eyes. She puffed out a breath, fogging up a small circle, and pressed her lips to it. Then she was gone. A cloud of smoke trailed after her the way most things did, and then there was nothing but the wet sound of tires on the soaked street. I watched the rain cover the tracks, watched the black asphalt forget her in a way I knew I never would.

I wondered if she ever wished the rain could touch her. If the rain was ever sad that it couldn't.

Every Room

CAITLYN SIEHL

I used to walk straight-spined
out of every room that wouldn't
have me.

Now I only want the smell
of your hair on my pillow,
your spoiled milk in
the fridge.
Another ruined thing I can't
throw away.

I don't care what it means
to stay after the movie ends,
to fall asleep in the dark
instead of going home to
a fridge with no eggs
and a bed with no body.

I love you and it means
something.
I love you and it means
I'll never forgive you.
Means I'll always forgive you.

Get Up

RAQUEL FRANCO

I SAT ON THE FLOOR OF MY MOTHER'S BATH-
room, watching her put on her mascara in front of the mirror,
my legs pulled into my chest, head resting on my knees. She
stepped back to inspect her work, then leaned in to apply another
coat.

Looking past her, I stared at her reflection. She was so beautiful,
all raven hair, brown skin, and delicate curves. More beautiful than
anyone I'd ever seen on TV. Her face wore her heritage perfectly:
high, edged cheekbones from her Cherokee mother, intense eyes and
Cupid's-bow lips from her African American/Caucasian father. Her
looks drew stares from men and glares from women. Not only did
people stare, but they always found themselves eager to unveil her
nationality. "What are you?" they'd ask. She'd wave her hand to shoo
them away, telling them she was Hispanic.

I was raised being told I was also Latina. I am in part, due to my
Columbian father, but I'd later find out there was more to my origin
story and to why she never owned up to her heritage. Growing up

as the only light-skinned girl in an all-black school, she never fit in. Girls bullied her for being "high yellow." For her, being Latina was the easiest and safest answer, an answer that wasn't followed by pain.

She was wearing a red silk robe, a glass of red wine sitting on the counter beside her. I loved stealing that robe and wearing it to bed. The muscles of her calves flexed as she leaned forward, lean and sinewy, but not because she worked out. It was rare I would take note of her body. It was always her face. She didn't need all that makeup, but she wore it even if she had no plans to leave the house. She always wanted to look her best, "just in case."

"I love you, Mama." I was nine. My mother was my best friend. It was just her and me against the world.

"Thank you, baby. I love you more."

"Where are you going?" I asked.

"Out with Patrick." She got down low and held my chin up, inspecting my face, searching for her own features. "Reese, you'll learn one day that boys were built to chase. You have to send them on a hunt, or they'll find something else to go after." I must have looked confused, and she continued. "I'm going to tell you a secret. A few weeks ago, Patrick was supposed to pick me up for dinner, and that man had the nerve to stand me up. I waited fifteen minutes for him before I left the house and went out with my girlfriends. I don't wait around for anyone. Tonight, we'll see if he redeems himself."

She stood up and continued her work. Before she left, she bent over my canopy bed to tuck me in, her face all movie star and ready to impress. She took my small fingers inside her palm and began to pray like she always did.

"Lord, we thank you for our strength. We thank you for watching over us, and I thank you for Reese. May you bless her with sweet dreams and sweet sleep."

Smiling, I replied, "Amen."

She kissed me on the forehead and rubbed my back, watching as my eyes fluttered closed. That night, I fell asleep knowing I wanted to be just like my mother.

"Reese, can you refill this for me?" Rolling my eyes, I got up and fetched the oversized jug of wine from the kitchen. I filled up her coffee cup, the one with my tiny purple palms painted on it and "Happy Mother's Day" written with fingers that were just learning to scrawl.

Again I sat on her bathroom floor, watching her get ready, legs pulled up to my chin. She used the same blush, the same mascara, the same eyeshadow. To the naked eye, she also looked the same. Her face had not allowed the years to pass. She stood back, inspecting her work. She put down her foundation and grabbed the eyelash curler, an implement I never understood. She squinted her left eye, opened the curler, and clamped down on her lash line. Watching this, I could feel my own lashes being pinched, and it made me cringe.

My stomach grumbled. I had barely eaten dinner the night before, and my breakfast cereal sat untouched on the kitchen table. "I think Eric is avoiding me. We usually pass notes all day, and it's been a few days. I think—"

"Reese, how many times have I told you? You have to play hard to get," she interrupted, looking down at me, irritated.

I looked down and sighed. "I know." I had known that would be her response, and I also knew I was not going to tell her that I'd already written him.

Secretly, Eric and I had been meeting every day behind the school to make out. I never wanted it to end. Tucked away in the corner of an emergency exit, we explored each other's mouths. In class, I'd watch the hands on the clock tick by until they reached three o'clock, when the bell would release me. My stomach fluttered with butterfly wings. I checked his earlier note to examine his handwriting one more time. I wanted to tell my mother all about it. I wanted her to know that he made me feel like flying. I wanted her to know I was in love. But Mom didn't believe in flying. You had to be caught, and he had to work to catch you. I knew she was right. She was always right. Mama would say "I told you so."

"Relax. Walk with your head high and shoulders back. Laugh, smile, and act like you haven't noticed, and then when he does reach out—and he will—don't write back."

I scrunched my eyebrows, eyebrows identical to my mother's, dark and thick. One of the few features that we shared. We also shared the same Cupid's-bow mouth and long fingers made to play the piano, though neither of us ever played. Our skin, although not the same tone, was soft and blemish-free. I always wondered if life would bear me the same gift of never aging.

I whined, "It's really hard not to."

Patrick poked his head into the bathroom. "Hey, I gotta go to work. Not sure when I'll get home. I'll see you guys later." He was not a man of many words. He kissed me on top of my head and slipped out.

Patrick was now my stepdad. I always felt this small but sharp stab in my stomach when I thought of him. When they got married, with me as their only witness, my mother was four months pregnant with my brother. After the ceremony, which felt like a puzzle being put together of which I was no longer a piece, I went into the pastor's bathroom and spilled tears onto the laminate floor, knowing that from then on, I was going to be the only one to clean them up. I'd lost my best friend and gained a stranger for a father, along with two stepsisters. It had been six years, and it still felt like it was just me. Me against the world. My mother and his kids, sitting at the dining room table, laughing and being all Brady Bunch while I was upstairs alone.

"Okay, I'll try to leave him alone." I stood up beside her and stared at our reflections in the mirror. She was as strong as her cheekbones and as mysterious as the pupils that hid inside the night of her eyes. I looked awkward and weak standing next to her, not knowing how to carry these new, unfamiliar curves.

"You are beautiful, Reese. You don't need to wait for anyone or feel sad if they don't realize what you're worth," she said without looking at me.

I sighed. "I'm going to go to Megan's to pick her up for school."

She turned around abruptly, the wine sloshing in her mug. "Like that?"

I looked down at my baggy jeans and my oversized long-sleeved Levi's T-shirt. My long, curly black hair was in a ponytail with the ends pulled halfway through the loop. She hated my hair like this, natural and lacking effort. She preferred it blown dry and straight like a white girl's hair, even though she always told me white girls weren't prettier than me. This was my favorite outfit, hiding everything. My feelings, my body, and my identity. As much work as my mother put into her looks, I put nothing. The harder she tried, the less I cared about my own appearance. The little girl who once thought of her as the most beautiful thing in the universe now found all that effort trivial.

"Yeah," I replied, rolling my eyes. I needed to get out of there, fast, before the badgering started. I turned and walked out of her room while her voice lingered after me like the smell of fresh skunk.

"What if you run into Eric like that?! Put on some makeup!" I heard her yell.

"I won't! God, who cares?!" I screeched back at her, rushing down the steps.

The phone rang in the kitchen.

"Hello?"

"Reese?" Eric's voice sounded as distant on the other end as his lack of letters.

"Eric, hi," I replied too loudly. I heard my mother's voice inside my head: "Play hard to get." I lowered my voice and said, "It's been a while." Three days, five hours and however many minutes too long, I thought.

"Yeah . . . well. About that."

My face grew hot. I could feel my body breaking down already, assuming the worst, preparing for impact.

"I've kinda been talking to Megan, and even though I loved you, I want to see where it can go with her. I'm sorry."

My voice was caught somewhere between "even though I loved you" and "her." I squeezed my eyes shut and asked, "When did this happen?"

"I don't know."

Lips. I could feel his lips on mine.

"Why did this happen?" I asked.

His hands. His hands holding my face, the back of my head pressed against the brick wall.

"Reese, I don't know. I'm sorry, okay?"

Safe. His hands were the only place I felt safe. No, this was not okay.

"But you said you loved me. Why her?" Hot tears slid down my cheeks as I poured out words I later would regret. He refused to participate in any further conversation. Spewed more I-don't-knows and I'm-sorrys. I realized I was fighting a battle after the white flag had been raised. I didn't want the white flag. I was red. I was bleeding red. Accepting defeat, I said goodbye and hung up the phone. Then, as if my wounds could no longer hold themselves together, the dam broke. I crumpled to my knees and sobbed.

My mother came down the stairs and walked into the kitchen, her face stern. I was witness to her disapproval of my seemingly arbitrary emotions.

"What is wrong with you?" she snapped.

I was choking on my tears.

"Reese. What is wrong with you?" she demanded.

"He … He … He broke up with me." My sobs swelled as I heard the reality come out of my mouth.

"Reese. Get up." She was standing above me, looking down on me. "Don't be weak. Stop crying."

"Mama, I love him. He's the first boy I have ever loved." I wanted her to hold me. To tell me everything was going to be okay. To tell me he'd come back. Tell me anything that would fill this gripping emptiness beneath my ribs.

"Go to your room if you're going to cry like that. Otherwise, pull yourself together, wash your face, and go to school." She walked around me and began putting the dirty dishes in the dishwasher.

With each minute that passed, her saying nothing, I felt more alone. I unfolded myself from the linoleum floor and walked into the bathroom down the hall. I looked at myself in the mirror, the rims of my eyes red, strands of my hair disheveled and frizzed. No effort, just some girl. I asked myself, "Will I ever be as beautiful as her? Will I ever be as strong? Will it always be this way?"

❦

Eleven years have passed since that day. Whether she felt sorry for me, I don't know, but she did try to help me get Eric back. She applied my makeup just the same as hers, Chanel, Elizabeth Arden, and L'Oreal painted all over my face. She straightened my hair and helped me pick out the perfect outfit. It was the first time I believed my mother when she told me I looked beautiful. She told me, "Never let them see you cry. Hold your head high. Know you are the prettiest girl in the room, and if you don't feel it, fake it." She taught me to walk straight-spined out of every room that wouldn't have me, even hers. I channeled the strength of my mother for much of my life.

My mother is no longer strong. My mother is no longer beautiful. My mother is no longer here. I watched her unravel. Her evening cocktail to take the edge off turned into wine instead of coffee for breakfast, then rum-and-diet for lunch and back again. She thought no one noticed. We all did. Patrick, my little brother, my stepsisters.

I watched her drink every night in front of the television; watched it turn from every night to every day and night; watched her get a DUI driving my siblings to school; watched her lose her home, her husband, her children, and her looks. I watched the woman I wanted to become turn into the woman I couldn't stand to be near. I never knew mountains could be unmade, but I guess if the earth shakes hard enough, it all turns to dust.

❦

The last time I went to see her, she was sitting on the couch, rail-thin, leg restlessly swinging, holding that damn oversized green plastic cup with the straw protruding from her rum-and-diet. I didn't know what to say. I had been out of words to say to her for quite some time. My visits, few and far between, originated from guilt. She was my mother. I had a feeling that her days were numbered, and when I was filled with the thought of regretting not seeing her, I'd stop by. My stomach was heavy with discomfort and anger. Sadness willed itself to stay down. She was watching Maury or some other daytime TV show I hated, adding even more to my discomfort. Yesterday's mascara and eyeliner were smudged around her eyes. I shifted in my seat, trying to angle my vision away from her kitchen, and my nose from the smell. The counter was piled high with mail and weeks of dirty dishes. Dishes I figured I'd scrub later, after she had passed out. Knowing she wouldn't clean up after herself made me even angrier. Knowing she was all alone here with this mess made me sad.

Unable to process my whirlwind of emotions, I told her I had to go.

She smiled. "Okay."

I stood and leaned over to hug her small frame, feeling like I was the adult and she was the child, and I left, leaving behind the dishes I had told myself I'd wash.

When I got the call, I was at a restaurant with my friends. The nurse said I needed to come to the hospital. I can't recall the details of what she said, but I was frantic. Something in me knew this was it. My mother was going to die. Although I knew this day would come sooner rather than later, nothing had prepared me for the day I lost my mother.

"I have to go. My mother is in the hospital." I didn't explain. I grabbed my things and walked out into the night. My best friend, Julia, ran after me and said she would drive me to the hospital. Within minutes of arriving, the doctor came into the waiting room to tell me she was gone. Her body had shut down. It couldn't fight for her any longer. They asked me if I wanted to say good-bye. Crying, I said no.

"Are you sure?" asked the doctor.

"Yes. She's not there anymore." I believed. I hoped she was in heaven, and the truth was I couldn't bear to see her. Lifeless. Dead. I couldn't say—didn't want to say—good-bye.

Julia took me home, we crawled into my bed with our clothes on, and she lay with me till I cried myself to sleep.

The next time I was in my mother's apartment, I was going through all her things, crying and wishing I wasn't doing it alone. Grief crippled rational thought, and I threw most everything away. I just wanted it to be over as quickly as possible. Among the mess and dirt and filth, I found all her makeup in a bathroom drawer—perfectly organized. Rows and rows of blush, bronzer, and eyeshadows. The vision of a little girl with her legs pulled into her chest on the bathroom floor flooded my mind, her eyes filled with wonderment as she watched the person she believed was the most put-together woman, put herself together. I clenched my eyes shut, tears escaping. My stomach churned, and I felt my fingers grabbing the lipstick. I ignored my crimson-rimmed eyes and mess of curls, removed the cap, and painted my mouth cherry red. I continued to apply her makeup just as she had all those years. Maybe I could hide behind it, just as she had. Maybe I could appear strong. I set her blush compact down and searched for her in the mirror. My eyes were as empty as the room. Anger began to fill the spaces, and I furiously removed the mask I had just created. I threw all the makeup in the trash can, already close to overflowing with empty rum bottles, dirty paper towels, and Taco Bell wrappers. I saved only a photo album, a handkerchief, and her bible.

٭٭٭٭

"Reese, it's time to say good-bye," my stepsister whispers, pulling me from my thoughts. She gently places her hand on my shoulder as if she's afraid she'll break me.

I sigh heavily. I should be crying, but I think I left all my tears in my bed. I stand and smooth my black dress, blink my dry eyes, and will them to stay open. I don't want to do this. I don't want the last years to have been real, but they were. My stepfather stands in the back of the room, stoic, but the red rims of his eyes reveal otherwise. A charge of love for him rises up in me, but I am tired and do not approach him. I am tired of all these people. I am tired of hearing "I am so sorry" and "You look just like her." It's making me want to vomit.

I walk down the aisle to sit with my family, passing rows of teary strangers dressed in black. The preacher opens his mouth and I hear nothing he says. I stare at her photo. Here in this picture, she is still the most beautiful thing in the room. She taught me how to catch a man, how to catch his eye, how never to wait. Taught me how to be without them, but not without her. I always wanted to grow up and be like her, but those days are gone. I am twenty-four, and I am a woman without her mother. I have no children with her eyes. I have no husband she'd be proud that I caught. No more chances to show her I can get it right.

Out of the corner of my eye, I see my brother's head drop. He is sobbing. These are the first tears I have seen on his face since he was a baby in my arms. After all that has happened, it's his tears that kill me and now I, too, am sobbing. I guess the rivers had yet to run dry.

I want to fall to the floor. "This isn't fair," I think. "My brother doesn't deserve to lose his mother. My grandmother, at the back of the room, ready to escape, doesn't deserve to lose her daughter. God, why?! I need my mother! She was the strongest person I know. How will I ever trust the ground I stand on after this?!"

Then I hear her voice. "Get up."

I blink. I hate you. I hate you for not being there. I hate you for wasting so much time putting on makeup. I hate you for choosing alcohol over us.

"Get up, Reese," I whisper. I will be strong, and I will walk straight-spined out of this room.

Less Is Not Always More

RAQUEL FRANCO

We've been drifting so long
I can't remember
what love tastes like,
what hunger feels like,
all hands and grasp
and ravish.
What tore the longing
from your eyes?
Our arms less hold
and more crossed,
inch by inch,
day by day,
moving to the other side
of the bed.
Hours spent
in the same room,
on the same couch
less together
and more stranger.
This new practice,
this daily drift,
has made this unraveling,
this unloving,
harder to find
our way back.

Stay with Me

COURTNEY PEPPERNELL

*W*HEN I WAS EIGHT YEARS OLD, MY mama told me I could be anything I wanted. If I wanted to design dresses or fight fires or count books or fly to the moon, I could. All I had to do was wish as hard as I could, and it would come true. Last year, when my girlfriend, Lena, died, I wished that she would come home.

She didn't.

Willowdale exists under thick layers of snow this time of year. It's an isolated Colorado town near the Utah border, hidden by frost-dusted mountains and connected to the outside world with just one long, winding highway. The winter sky is often cloudy, the sun rarely daring to show itself, and I prefer it that way. I arrived at Uncle Buck's homestead shortly after the funeral, determined to get as far away from Boston as possible. I had hoped that the memories would not follow, that I would be able to forget what I lost that day as the sun was setting.

Ironically, my uncle's ranch bears the name Mournstead. I have refused to look at the timber-framed sign above the driveway since the first day I read it. If you mourn a person, it means you've said goodbye, and how do you say goodbye to the love of your life?

When I first arrived, the late spring sun shone brightly in the clear sky, and I hated it, for with it came a shadow I was trying hard to lose. And a visible sunset. Back then, the townsfolk of Willowdale wanted to get to know me. There was nowhere I could go without someone asking how I was or if I needed any help. I didn't know how to explain that the only thing I wanted was buried back in Boston. After a while, I think they grew to see my shadow, too. How it would follow me past the coffee shop, the diner, or the florist. How it would sit with me in the local bar and drink with me. I knew they whispered about Buck's niece: how sad for her, she seemed so lost, so distant. Now, the more time passes, the more it seems I am no closer to losing this shadow than I am to losing the sun.

I walk into Bobby's Diner and slide into an empty booth. The waitress appears beside me and pours a cup of coffee.

"How you doing, Madge?" I ask. It's always easier to ask this of someone else before they can ask me.

"Fine, hon," she replies. "But I can feel this cold in my bones."

I smile, folding my arms across the table. "Can I get the usual?"

"Mac and cheese with peas," she replies, grinning, and she makes her way to the kitchen.

I fiddle with the creamer and the sugar on the table before noticing a couple in another booth, their heads bent close together, sharing a milkshake. I used to share milkshakes with Lena, pretending to be mad when she would drink most of it. I run my fingers along the scar on my forehead. Scars heal; the skin weaves itself over the wound and leaves a faint mark in its place. I've spent months wondering if the hole in my heart will do the same.

Though it was early spring when the accident happened, it had been snowing that afternoon, and Lena was driving. I had told her we were going to the movies, but instead I was taking her to our favorite place by the lake. The ring was sitting inside my jacket, and I could feel it burning its way into my skin. Sam Smith was playing on the radio, and Lena turned up the volume, dancing behind the wheel, reaching over and touching my face every time we heard our favorite line. Neither of us saw the tree branches in the middle of the road.

My memory is fragmented, but pieces still float back to me in flashes. The way the vehicle flipped like a ship tossed between waves, the metal crunching together, before ploughing into the surrounding trees. The smell of rubber burnt into the tar road, tires screaming into the silence. A hand on my face. The stillness of the air around us, and the realization that Lena was not moving, not breathing. But what I remember the most is the sun, how it seemed to disappear faster than normal, shrinking below the horizon as though it did not want to bear witness.

Lena and I used to lie under the covers on Sunday afternoons and talk about what our children would look like. We talked about the adventures we would have and about getting married in the mountains. She was so poised, elegant, in control—an anchor to my sails. Since losing her, I have been swept away, lost in an unforgiving current. I can't remember what love tastes like, any more than I can remember the feeling of her hands as they ran through my hair, pulling me closer to her.

Lena was taken from me in the dusk as the sun was setting, linking the sun with my nightmare. The light casts a shadow of grief, a relentless reminder of what I no longer have. It is no longer a source of hope, but rather a cause of darkness across my heart. Everything about the sun reminds me that Lena is no longer with me. I have avoided the sunset since the accident. I refuse to be outside at dusk, to listen to it, absorb it, feel it wrapping around me. For me, the sunset is a constant reminder, a magnet pulling me back into the worst moments of my life.

The sun has started its descent, so I push away my half-finished plate and empty my pockets of dollar bills. At the counter, Madge is slicing a pie for the couple in the front window—key lime, I think. She watches me gather my things, and I smile at her as I walk out to the parking lot. I sit in my truck for a moment, staring at the couple in the booth and playing with my keys.

Knock, knock, knock.

My keys tumble to the floor and I look out the window. Melded with my reflection is a familiar face. Norah. Standing outside, head tilted in the way she usually looks at me: with playful interest. I roll down the window, then retrieve my keys from the floorboards, hitting my head on the steering wheel as I come up.

"The sun is setting." She is grinning.

"I know." I reply, rubbing my head.

"You better get going then," she says, drumming her fingers on the side of the truck. She mimics the sound of an eerie voice: "The dusk is coming."

"Are you always this insensitive?" I ask.

She thinks for a moment. "Not in calving season. That's enough to make even your uncle cry."

I look away from her, half smiling, before turning the key in the ignition and causing the truck to roar to life.

"Hey," she says, and I glance over at her.

"How about you stay, have dinner with me?"

"I just ate," I respond.

She bites her lip. "Tomorrow then? I'll see you at the usual place?"

I fight the pounding in my chest, the same way I have fought it for the last few months. For so long, my heart has been motionless. What once gave me joy and hope is lost. What once made my heart race is gone. But with Norah, it's different. Every time Norah is around, I think about what I have, not what I've lost.

"Tomorrow then. At the fence line."

Her face lights up. "Tomorrow."

As I pull the truck out onto the road, I look back through my review mirror, but Norah's gone.

When I first arrived at Mournstead, I didn't have a clue about working on a farm. Now I can tell you when the storms are coming in, just from the smell in the air. I can tell you how to wean a calf from its mother, how to manage pastures, and how many shades of blue the wide-open sky holds. I plunge the wooden stake into the ground, hammering the top so that it stays in place. The new wire I have is dozens of metres long, and if I don't get the fence fixed, our herd will wander into neighboring property. I can feel the sweat on the back of my neck, under the layers of my thick coat. I hear my name, and I look up to see Norah standing at the fence, that same playful smile on her face.

117

"Where's your horse?" I ask.

"Nearby," she replies. "You coming to William's birthday bash?"

"How old is he now?"

"Sixty. You owe me a dance."

I pull the wire from the ground, starting to untangle it.

Norah waits for me to answer. When I don't, she looks out at the mountains around us, the pale blue sky scattered with clouds. "It's so beautiful today. The sun is so bright."

I busy myself with the wire. I can't bring myself to make conversation, and I hate myself for it. Norah has been kind to me and patient, even on the days when there was nothing more I wanted than to drown in silence. But how do you explain to someone that you don't have any idea how to put yourself back together again? I finally turn to tell Norah that I'm sorry, that yes, the sky is beautiful, but she's no longer there.

William Grant has been my uncle's neighbor and friend for more than three decades. The party is in his barn, which is filled with fairy lights, a live band, and what seems like everyone in Willowdale.

Callum Ryder, a ranch hand on the Grant farm, ambles up to me and casually comments that I ought to enter the Spring Rodeo this year. He looks down at me, grinning like a coyote, knowing full well I have no talent.

"That's more your area, Cal. Although I do wonder, will they have horses with legs long enough for you?" I quip. I sip a beer, staring out at the crowded barn.

"Oh, come on, Skylar, you'd be just fine at it," he says.

"Norah would probably think it's the funniest thing in the world."

Callum looks at me quizzically. "Who's—?"

"Speaking of," I say, noticing Norah at the doorway of the barn. I pat Callum's chest and make my way through the already-drunk partiers to Norah.

"Better late than never," I say. "Although for one of the Grants' ranch hands, you sure did miss the start time."

"Wasn't sure what to wear," she responds, her eyes sparkling.

She's wearing a blue dress that cuts away just above her knees. Her hair is braided on the side, and she wears a delicate flower crown. My heart is pounding in a way I can't control. Norah can draw me closer to her in the moments I feel most vulnerable, and I have no idea how she does it.

"You look beautiful," I say, and my own words catch me off guard.

She brings her hand to her chest. "Is Skylar Thompson complimenting me?"

"Don't get used to it," I reply, and I smile. But the moment is fleeting, and I arrive at the same argument I have been having with myself since the instant I met Norah. When you lose someone you love so dearly, how do you find the courage to smile again, to be able to laugh, and to admire a beautiful woman standing in front of you without feeling guilt?

"So, that dance," Norah says, reaching for my hand and pulling me to her, like a new anchor.

I wonder if I am allowed to dance with someone else, but I don't stop Norah. I allow her to take my hand in hers. The fire between our fingers, the longing not to let go, is almost overwhelming. She leads me to the corner, where the light is barely touching the wooden barrels. The band plays a song I don't recognize, and the room has fallen away. Norah wraps her arms around my neck and draws me closer. I inhale deeply: coconut and pine trees. I haven't held someone in so long that I've almost forgotten what it's like to have a heart beating against mine. Even so, there's a part of me that's screaming to push her away, to run back to the memories I have been trying so hard to hold onto. Memories of Lena, of the life we once had. Yet there is something holding me in place, and as I dance with Norah, our feet stepping gently through the hay, I wonder if it's possible to be found when you've been so lost.

Winter on Mournstead, like any ranch, is mostly about maintenance. My uncle has fifteen other ranch hands across his three-thousand-acre property. The pastures are all under heavy layers of snow, so the first thing I do each day is feed the livestock. Then I chop firewood, and either ride out in the rig or take my horse, Scout, to survey the property or fix any of the fences that have come down. Fences are always falling. They're like people, always needing to be fixed. Today is no different: I've spent most of the afternoon along the northern parts of Mournstead, fixing fence posts. My uncle thinks coyotes have been chewing away to break into the property, but if you ask me, the wooden stakes are so old they're rotting, like memories.

Lost in my own memories and the rotting posts, I blink a few times when I realize the sun is sinking, the rays slipping past the peaks of the mountain range. I mount Scout, and we ride back toward the homestead. Looking back at the deepening sky, I find myself leading her into a gallop, racing against the fading sunlight. I tuck her into the barn and run to the house, making it inside just before the rays disappear and the twilight spreads its purple blanket.

My uncle's house is full of the trinkets and memories of my late aunt, but my favorites are the old license plates he has nailed up along the walls. Together they collected all fifty states, and he's proud of that. I sit at the kitchen counter for a moment, fiddling with the caps of discarded beer bottles. I wonder why Norah didn't show up at the fence line like she usually does, and I am confused about the ache in my chest.

When I first met Norah last summer, I was down by the river that borders my uncle's property and the Grants' ranch to the south. She told me she was new to town and had taken a job at the Grants', mustering the horses. There was something in the way she spoke, like I had heard her voice before, and it unnerved me. Norah started just showing up—always in places I was alone. For a while, I thought it was because she knew about my loss and that maybe I needed some-one: a friend, a light to guide me.

I throw away the caps and move to the kettle. I wait for it to boil, then drown the tea bag waiting in my mug. I hear my name being called. I go to the front window, pull the curtain aside, and look out at the porch. Norah is standing at the door.

"Where were you?" she asks as I throw open the door. "I waited by the fence."

"You were too late," I reply.

She sighs, folding her arms across her heavy coat. "When are you going to start living again, Skylar? You can't live like this."

"I can live any way I want to," I reply, agitated. Increasingly, Norah has been intent on keeping me out at dusk, and I don't understand why this is so important to her.

"What, constantly in fear of the setting sun?"

"You were supposed to meet me earlier," I snap. "You didn't have a problem before, so why are you now so insistent on staying out as the sun goes down?"

"You can't blame me," she replies. "Wanting to have dinner with you, or wanting to watch the sun set behind the mountains with you. Does it really sound so bad?"

"I just can't." I choke as I speak. What I can't tell her is that it sounds perfect. To spend a day—and night—with Norah. To not be afraid. But I have already lost someone I loved to the fading light of the day.

"Come on, Sky," she says. I picture how incredible she'd look in the fading colors of the day, the way they'd make her skin glow, and reflect off her long hair. "Let's go for a walk and listen to the nightfall."

"I said no," I reply, angry now. "Why can't you just accept me for who I am?"

I slam the door on her, not wanting her to see the tears that have sprung into my eyes, and I rush up the stairs. I fall into a heap on my bed, my heart pounding in my ears, holding on to my pillow as if it might save me. There is a knock at my door, and I wonder if Norah has come to apologize, to reassure me that I can stay in the shadows for as long as I want. The knocking continues.

"Norah, just leave me alone!"

"Uh, Skylar, it's me." My uncle's voice cracks as he says my name.

I push myself off the bed and open the door. Uncle Buck stands there with a backpack and rifle slung over his shoulder.

"You going somewhere?" I ask.

"Heading up to the cabin with Will," he replies. "One last hoo-ha for his birthday."

"Sure," I reply, and I hastily wipe my eyes. "Snowfall is easing up, but it's still cold. Be careful."

"You know we always are," he says. "Ranch hands will be here if you need anything."

"I can handle it for a few days."

"Sky," he says softly, "are you . . . ?" He trails off, his eyes cast to the floor.

"Am I what?"

"It's nothing," he says, but he looks uncomfortable. My uncle is a quiet man. He speaks with gestures, not words. For the first month I was at Mournstead, I had nightmares. My uncle didn't say anything; instead, he just let the dogs sleep in my room. When I fell off Scout for the first time, again he didn't say anything, just wrapped up my wrist in a bandage. Looking at him now, I know he is struggling to find the words.

"It is something," I reply. "Because you're looking at me like we just lost your prize bull."

"The party the other night." He gathers himself. "In the corner of the barn, you was just dancing by yourself is all."

I stand in my bedroom doorway, my body rigid, while he gently places his hand on my head, brushing my scar with his thumb. He mutters something about seeing me when he returns home, and to look after myself. I hear him leave through the back door; it closes with a click. Without thinking, I go back downstairs, throwing open the front door, searching for Norah. The gathering evening is cold and indigo. A chill runs through my body when I see there is only one set of footsteps in the snow: mine.

The storm comes in quickly. It rolls in with thick, dark clouds and hurls rain at the land as though it is trying to wash all the snow away. The flames are crackling in the fireplace as I sit under a blanket reading a Farm & Ranch catalog. A sharp crack of thunder causes the entire house to shudder. There is another crack, and everything is illuminated by lightning. I can hear the horses neighing and stomping their hooves, panicking out in the barn, and I put on my coat and boots, readying myself to go comfort them. As I open the door to the house, the barn door flies open and Scout bolts.

"Scout!" I yell frantically. I grab a flashlight and charge outside.

The wind is howling as I fight my way through rain and sleet, following her. I curse myself for not padlocking the barn and pray none of the other horses escape their stables. I push past branches, my heart in overdrive as I count each hoofprint leading toward the riverbank. The rain has turned the icy river into slush. I hear Scout whinny, and I squint through the dark in her direction. I just make out her outline on the bank, making her way past a cluster of trees toward the path back to the barn.

"Good girl. Stay there, I'm coming for you."

I move to climb over a fallen tree, but my jeans catch on a broken branch, and I tumble forward into the bank. The river meets me with a rush of cold water and mud. It's angry, and pierces my skin like needles. I am swept under briefly and try to find my footing. But the rain has made the water rise, and it's too deep. I reach out, clutching tree roots, pulling myself upward. My arms feel frozen, my lips trembling as I try to focus my attention on pulling myself up, and not on how cold the water is.

"Pull yourself up, Skylar."

"Norah?" I call above the rain. My fingers struggle to keep a grip on the branches. My hair is tangled with mud. I can just see Norah, standing on the bank, but my vision is blurry, as though she is scattered by the moonlight.

"Norah, help me!" I yell, reaching for her hand. "It's too slippery. I can't move!"

My words are barely audible as the rain pelts down.

"You have to get up, Skylar," she says. "No one else can do this for you. It's time to get up."

"Norah!" I scream again. I'm so confused. Why isn't she helping me?

But as quickly as she appeared, she is gone, and I dig my fingers into the bank, pulling myself forward through the slush and soil. The rain has lightened up, but I'm shivering violently, and I can barely feel my arms and legs. As I lie coughing on the bank, I feel Scout's nose push into my chest. I bite down on my lip, searching for strength, and I pull myself up to standing. I bury my face in her mane, tangled and wet from the rain.

"Let's go home," I whisper.

The skies have been clear for weeks, the days have grown warmer, the snow has melted into thin banks beside roads and streams. Spring will be returning soon, and it's meant to bring hope, yet I feel like I am the only person it won't return to. I haven't seen Norah since the night of the storm. I know she is someone I dreamed up. All the hours spent at the fence line, me working, her talking about life and love, trying to bring normality and sense back into my life. I realize that the woman with the playful smile who was constantly a pain in my side, she was the one who convinced me that life was worth living again. But she wasn't even real.

When I tell Uncle Buck about Norah, he takes a bottle of whiskey from the shelf and pours me a glass. As I examine the amber liquid, I understand that grief can manifest into something beyond imagination. I can still feel Norah's hand. I can still hear her laugh as it would ring out into the sky around us. If Norah brought the beat back to my heart, but she never existed in the first place, how can I be sure my heart is even truly beating?

⁂

I weave the wire through the fence post, standing back to admire my work. I squint up at the sun. It has started to lower itself toward the mountains, retiring for the day. I pile the rest of the stakes into the back of the rig, tightening down the load with ropes. The air is crisp, and flocks of geese have started to return. I watch them fly over for a moment, wondering if I, too, will be able to return home someday. There is a screech of tires on the road, followed by the sound of glass shattering. I jump into the rig and peel away from the fence, driving up toward the road, to the smoke now rising into the blue sky.

There is a vehicle upside down, small flames licking the rear of the engine. My stomach ties itself in knots as I stumble toward the wreck, reaching for my phone and dialling 9-1-1.

"There's been an accident on Old Bronson Road," I inform the operator.

"All emergency vehicles are deployed to a fire in Billy's Creek," the operator replies. "I'll send a patrol unit as soon as possible."

"That's the next town over!" I am frantic. "That will take forever!"

"I'm sorry, miss, we'll do everything we can."

I make my way to the door of the vehicle and crouch down, looking inside. There is a woman on the driver's side, lying limp against the steering wheel.

"Hey!" I say. "Can you hear me?"

One of the farmhands was involved in a bad tractor accident last fall. I can still see the blood. I still see Lena, not moving. I crawl through the window and over the glass, ignoring the shards pulling at my shirt, scraping my skin. I reach for the woman's shoulder, letting her know someone is there to help. She murmurs something, and when her head turns to me, I muffle the sound of my own panic.

"Norah?"

This can't be happening.

"My leg," she whimpers.

"But you're not real," I whisper, fighting the dread that crawls through my veins. The smell of gasoline and the heat are real. There is a popping sound, and I know the engine will explode at any minute.

The woman brings her hand to my face and with it, a sense of familiarity. She says, her breath short, "It's you."

My mind twists as I try to make sense of what's happening. Is this another vision, or does Norah truly exist?

I don't have time to decide.

"I have to get you out," I say. "I don't know if help is coming, but it's too dangerous to stay in here."

I fumble for my pocketknife and cut away at the seat belt. It snaps back, and I balance the woman, trying to get to the steering wheel, where her leg is trapped.

"Skylar," she blurts. "I have your ring."

The memory floods back in a flash of sunlight. Lena swerving around the tree debris, the vehicle losing balance on the icy road. Her arm reaching out and slamming into my chest, pushing me back against the seat. The glass shattering, the vehicle flipping, our bodies rolling with it until it finally crashes into the trees. The darkness swallowing us until my eyes flicker open and I feel the blood running down my face. The realization that Lena isn't moving, that her chest is still and her lips pale blue. The sun fading quickly through the smashed windshield and ending with the eruption of dusk. The sirens blaring through the street, drowning out the noise of the radio. The flashlights lighting up the sky like blue and red fireworks. The sound of police-radio chatter and approaching footsteps, someone calling for immediate medical assistance. Then a voice, soft and calm, telling me everything is going to be okay. That same familiar voice, begging me to hold on. The same hand reaching for my face, my hand, taking it gently. The shock sinking in over what I have lost, the darkness swallowing me again until I am in the back of an ambulance. But the hand has not let go. It is a warmth keeping me in this life, clutching at mine tightly. The voice filling the void, whispering for me to stay.

It was Norah.

"You were there," I choke.

"I've been looking for you," she whispers, and her eyes flicker, fighting to stay open.

"Stay with me," I say, and my hands start to shake as I fight to drive the steering wheel lever upward, to free Norah's leg. It moves and her leg drops, releasing her. I struggle to balance us both as I retract backwards out of the vehicle.

"This is going to hurt," I say, and I am nauseous and determined as I drag her through bent steel onto the open road. Norah's screams light up the trees and send birds fleeing into the sky. A ring box tumbles out onto the gravel. The same ring box I had with me the day Lena died. I peel off my coat, wrapping it tightly around Norah and dialling 9-1-1 again.

"I'm coming," I say to the operator. "I'm ten minutes from Willowdale Hospital. It'll be faster."

"Skylar," Norah murmurs against me. She is losing blood.

"Hold on," I say, pulling her up and wrapping her arm around my shoulder. "Just get to the truck." I half drag Norah, half drag myself, toward my rig.

In moments that feel like centuries, we race along the highway, Norah in and out of consciousness beside me.

"I found you," she says, defiant, but her breath is raspy and fading.

I look to her, glancing at her shaking leg, her jeans drenched with blood. I am not sure if I've done more harm than good.

"Just stay awake, Norah."

"You know my name."

I place my arm across her chest the same way Lena did for me, holding her in place, holding her in this life. "Stay with me," I say, the song filling the cabin of the truck even though the radio is off. "Just stay with me, please."

Her hand wraps around mine as I burn through the last miles toward the hospital. The sun has already begun to set, and soon we are driving through the dusk, the fading colors of the day splayed across the sky. The first time I have seen the sunset in a year, and I am with Norah. I need to make it; I won't let the dusk take someone else.

There is a painting on the wall near the nurses' station. It's of the sun setting behind the Rockies. The pinks and yellows are wrapped up in one another, captured in a moment that happens every day. I imagine what follows once the sun sinks low beyond the mountain range. The dusk approaches, filling the night air with the sound of crickets, then the moon rises and begins to shine as the sky darkens and the night falls. Such a beautiful farewell to the day, and I have missed so many of them.

The nurse appears from Norah's room and smiles at me.

"She's asleep, but you can see her now."

"Thank you," I murmur, and I brush past her into the room.

The curtains are drawn, the room dark aside from the lamp switched on beside the bed. Norah is asleep, her leg propped up on pillows and wrapped tightly in bandages. The machine beside her beeps in rhythm with her heart. I pull over the chair from the corner of the room and sit down next to her. I watch as her chest rises and falls.

Norah was the responding officer on the afternoon of the accident. She assisted the paramedics, and held my hand when I screamed as they cut me from the vehicle. She stroked my hair in the back of the ambulance as the paramedic administered morphine. She whispered for me to hold on as I cried out for Lena. She was there the day my whole world came crashing down around me, and while she was looking for me in the months after I ran away from the memories, I was having my own memories of her.

"You saved my life," I whisper, and the tears spill down my face, splashing onto my lap.

People experience loss all the time. They lose people they love, things they love, and they lose themselves. In that loss, there is always something that brings them back home again, and Norah is mine. I place my hand over hers, running my thumb gently over her skin.

She is real.

The tears continue to run down my face as I try to think of an explanation, but like grief, maybe this doesn't need an explanation at all. After a moment, Norah's fingers wrap around mine, and she squeezes my hand. Holding me to this life, as much as I am holding her.

⚬❧⚬

The snow has melted away, and poppies are springing up from the ground where they were hiding for the winter. Scout grazes in the field with the other horses, enjoying the sunlight. Norah appears on the front porch, handing me a mug of coffee. There is a strangeness to fate, to things we cannot explain. There is no answer for why I could see Norah, as much as there is no answer for why she felt so real, but it doesn't change the fact that it happened.

"I thought you would still be out on the fences," Norah says.

I take the coffee from her. "The sun looks so beautiful setting across these mountains," I say. "And I wanted to check on you. How's your leg?"

"I'm still alive," she replies, and she smiles. "Thanks to you."

I turn from her, concentrating on the sky changing color, not knowing how to explain what I feel for her. How do I tell her that I am alive because of her?

"How did you find me?" I ask.

She looks out toward the mountains. "I looked for you under the contact details we had from the incident report, but the phone we had on record was disconnected."

"Yes," I reply. "I left Boston shortly after Lena's funeral."

"I contacted Lena's parents and they mentioned you had moved out to Colorado, to your uncle's ranch."

I haven't mentioned Lena's name to anyone in so long, afraid that just saying it would be enough to drag back all the old memories I've been running from. Her name has been woven into my instability, as though it has made all this unraveling justified. But hearing it on Norah's lips brings a new kind of balance, like this new practice, this daily drift, calling me back home.

"I can't explain it," Norah says. "I was compelled to find you,

Skylar."

"Because of the ring?"

"After the accident, I got called out to a hit and run. My responding officer and I made errors, and the victim died at the scene. I felt like it was my fault, that I no longer had the right to be a police officer. I was meant to protect lives, and I failed."

"You can't control what happens," I say to her. "Fate works in ways we don't understand."

"It was more than that. Just inch by inch, day by day, I felt as though I was losing myself and my purpose in this world. Then one afternoon, I came across your ring in the evidence locker, and I realized it had never been returned to you. I knew then that I needed to do that."

I look at her. "I never thought I would see it again. I thought it had been lost to the dusk. I've been so afraid of watching the sunset ever since the accident."

Norah gently closes the space between us, and I feel the heat of her skin as she pulls me closer to her, dragging me in from the current, keeping my sails steady, an anchor.

"Are you going to stay?" I barely manage.

"I want to stay," she whispers. "But I'm afraid."

I search her face for answers. Her eyes, glistening in the late afternoon sunshine; her hair draped over her shoulders; her skin soft like her smile. There is so much about her that I recognize, so much about her that feels familiar.

"I've seen you in my dreams, Skylar," she says. "They've felt so real, I'm not sure what to believe."

Could Norah have seen me the same way I've seen her? Have we both been so lost that the key to finding our way back has been in each other?

"Maybe they're not dreams," I respond softly. "Maybe they're memories."

She smiles, glancing out at the horses as they graze in the fields beyond the homestead.

"Stay with me," I say. "At least for a little while."

I lean on the railing, looking out to the surrounding mountains, how they seem to split open across the fields against the sky. For the first time since the day I arrived on this ranch, I look up at the timber-framed sign above the driveway. It reads Mornstead. As if only now, I am able to see it for what it really is. I found myself here not to mourn, but to return home to the morning. The sun begins to set between the trees, spilling golden light before us. It bounces upward toward my face, casting shadows beneath my eyes. But I am no longer afraid of it. Instead I breathe in the smell of the pine trees and the fading scent of the day. I feel Lena with me, disappearing with the setting light of the sun. Yet I also feel Norah as she gently takes my hand, and I know tomorrow we will watch another sunset.

Slowly, or maybe all at once, my heart has returned to the sun.

A Thousand Miles Away

Courtney Peppernell

The cabs were piling up in front of us, and we both knew if I didn't leave, I'd miss my flight again. So many tears shed at the departure gate, wondering if I would ever see you again. You were crying, and I didn't know if it was because you wanted me to stay or you wanted the leaving to turn back into the missing. Somehow the missing was getting easier. I kissed you and I thought that if I could just stay here, outside the airport, with all the noise of the traffic, it would somehow be enough. But things are never enough, not when it comes to us. How we have danced the same dance for years and wrapped all the distance in I love yous from far away, sealed with our greatest fears. But you are the person I love, and so I don't know what to do. Because I love someone a thousand miles away, and I don't know how not to.

Wrapped in Distance

KOMAL KAPOOR

*T*HIS IS YOUR RESPONSIBILITY, PRIYA. You are the sister," my father said. "You know, she could be the one." He could barely contain his excitement. I couldn't believe I had to leave college in the middle of finals and drive eighty-five miles to my house for my brother's blind date.

"I have a really important paper due tomorrow," I said.

My mother regarded me in the rearview mirror, looking like she had smelled a bad piece of meat. "You work on papers every day. She will be a new member of the family. You don't want to meet her?"

"So what does she do?" I asked.

"Right now, she is at home." My mother glowed, her back straighter against the driver's seat. "Finished high school at fourteen. She is a year younger to you, got her MBA at nineteen. We should really have homeschooled you. But we didn't know—"

My father jumped in. "Why would we have homeschooled her? We might as well have stayed in India then."

I let them continue their argument as I stared at them. My mother looked old as she squinted at the traffic around her. She definitely shouldn't be driving anymore. It was always the old women who made a point of keeping their position behind the wheel. Old men knew better, or just died earlier. My thoughts drifted to the distance between my mother and me. The eighty-five miles, the generations and continents between her upbringing in India and mine here.

"Kaplan cannot be compared to UCLA," my father said.

"Kaplan?" I interrupted. "She got her degree from Kaplan? Isn't that one of those online programs?" There was no way someone could learn business skills without actually interacting with people. One point for me, zero for the future bride.

My mother now turned in her seat, making the car swerve a little to the right and causing my father to gasp. She ignored him and righted the car in the lane. "Yes, online. So smart. Didn't have to bother with all of your social events and all. What is this international thing anyway? You don't even do science anymore. Will you meet the President?"

"Probably. It'll take a few more months, though." I rolled my eyes and slurped my Diet Dr. Pepper, spilling a few drops on my sweater.

My mother shot me another look in the rearview mirror. "Anyway, she looks very pretty in her pictures on the internet. Very fair. A little short, but it is okay. She has good child-bearing hips." My father nodded along.

The thought of my parents checking out bodies of girls online for the delivery of their future grandbabies struck me as perverse. I took another sip of my drink and opened my textbook. Reading the small print was too difficult as my mother navigated the bumps and turns of the freeway, so I just stared at the lines, flipping a page occasionally in an effort to stay out of any conversation.

I walked into the house and stopped abruptly in the entryway. A four-foot statue of Ganesha greeted me, painted in rich tones of yellow, orange, and gold, and adorned with garlands of tiny white flowers and silver chains. A carved mouse sat at his feet, nibbling on a chestnut. "Nice addition, Mama," I said as my mother walked in behind me. She admired the statue as if it were a masterpiece she herself had slaved over for months.

"Oh yes, isn't it magnificent? You'll never believe we got it at a Chinese store downtown. First they sell Indian spices, now they are even making our gods. Pretty soon Ganesha will have *chinni* eyes too."

I ignored the racist comment; it wasn't worth the explanation. She smoothed out the invisible wrinkles on the white lace cloth underneath the statue and said, "I am just glad they delivered it in time for the dinner tonight."

"Why? Are these people really religious?" I asked.

I couldn't remember the last time my family had gone to the temple. Our prayer room didn't get much foot traffic either.

"What religious? We are Indian! This is what Indian people have in the house," she said, and walked into the kitchen to continue preparing dinner.

My father leaned over from the upstairs banister. "Priya, go see if Mama needs help with the food. She was up half the night cooking." I could smell cumin and onions being toasted.

"Need help, Mama?" I offered as I tried to sneak a fried *tikki* from the mound next to an array of chutneys. It was too hot, and I quickly dropped it, upsetting the arrangement and burning my fingers.

"Those are for the guests!" my mother screeched, and slapped my hand. "Stop causing trouble in the kitchen and go get ready. They'll be here in an hour. And dress normally!"

"Don't I always dress normally?" I mumbled, turning to leave.

"You know what I mean! Be decent. These aren't your American friends," she called out as I walked up the stairs.

I was hit by the smell of Cool Water wafting from my brother's room. Vijay must be out of the shower and drenching himself in his favorite cologne. I walked into his room. "So, *bhaiya*, what's this potential bride about? What happened to Nidhi?"

"Things didn't work out with her. I'm just going to let Papa and Mama pick. They know best," he said, adjusting his shirt collar. "If we were in India, that's how it would be."

The sixteen years of schooling in India had really made him the ideal son, right down to his dating choices.

"Um, I guess. I still can't believe she didn't want a one-on-one meeting first," I said. The odor of the Brylcreem he was combing through his hair fought with his cologne for attention.

"She is very traditional, wanted to meet with both families present," he said.

What was going on here? Had we transported back to India? "Oh, I thought she was born and raised here?"

"So what? All her relatives live here, even all her friends on Facebook are Indian."

I didn't know what to say to that. I could tell him that he was crazy to even consider marrying a stranger, that he had just reconfirmed my belief in never dating Indian guys. I settled with: "I gotta get ready." I walked out.

I stood in front of my closet, hoping an outfit would jump out at me. *Dress normally.* Dresses were definitely out of the question—too much skin. Tank tops, too low. Pleasing my mother was a lost cause. I realized all my makeup was back at the dorm. Makeup was probably too much for these genius-Indian-homeschoolers, anyway; having unmarried girls adorn themselves would be scandalous.

I finally settled on a turquoise sweater that was loose enough to cover any curves that may offend, and I paired it with some grey jeans that weren't too formfitting. I leaned in to examine myself more closely in the mirror. I knew my cropped hair would cause the usual scorn from my mother and elicit surprise from the traditionalists, but they'd just have to deal with it. I pushed a few wayward locks back into place and walked out of the room.

The doorbell rang and I hurried downstairs. My mother frantically flailed her arms, which I understood as her wanting me to come to the kitchen. "I have been looking for you! Okay, now don't make me ask you in front of them; make sure everyone has something to drink. And serve the snacks," she whispered with urgency, squeezing my arm as though it were dough to be rounded for a naan.

"Yes, Mama. Is what I'm wearing okay?" I whispered back.

After giving me a once-over, she said, "Push your hair out of your eyes."

She scuttled out of the kitchen as my father stood at the foot of the stairs. I glanced out from behind the kitchen sink while putting glasses of ice and cans of soda on a tray. My hands were getting clammy, and I grabbed a hand towel to wipe away the prints of sweat that I left on the tumblers. The guests were taking ages to hang up their coats. I wanted to get past the awkward introduction.

"Please come in. Let us have a seat." My father's voice boomed through the short hallway, deeper and more authoritative than usual.

The bride's father shuffled through behind him. "Yes, yes, of course, Sirji."

The Mehtas were a family of short people. The father's tight blue shirt hugged his stomach, and the buttons strained enough to show a gap, revealing his navel. His even-shorter wife trailed behind him, draped in a saree matching her husband's shirt. Behind them was the potential bride, Megha, barely five feet. Her silky black hair contrasted sharply with her pale skin and cascaded down her back. The hems of her maroon *salwar-kameez* were embroidered with gold sequins and miniature tear-shaped bells that glittered when the light hit them. There was the glint of a *bindi* on her forehead the same bronze as the bells on the *salwar*. Her hair was covered with a matching *chunni*, and her head was bent in the traditional bridal pose. Beneath all this, her eyes flitted back and forth, betraying her anxiety.

I looked away, somewhat embarrassed for scrutinizing her so and wondering why she would be nervous—all this was her idea. She must have done this a dozen times already, scouting the perfect groom. I noticed my mother giving her the full-body scan too. I could tell by Mama's alert eyes and the pinched corners of her smile that she could hardly contain her excitement as this jewel from India stepped into her living room. She always berated me about not wearing Indian clothes. The one saree she had forced upon me had hung in my closet for the past four years, unworn. I didn't even bother packing it for college even though she was sure I'd regret not having it. Such circumstances had yet to arise. Was I supposed to show up to happy hour at the college bar in a saree?

My father ushered everyone to the couches, and I took my place behind the granite counter. I looked down at the plate of cashew *burfis* lined with silver paper, wishing I could eat one. Instead, I put it on the tray next to the drinks and samosas, and walked toward the sofa.

"Priya, *beta*, what do you do?" Mr. Mehta asked me.

"Oh, she goes to UCLA right now. Doing International Relations," my mother jumped in. I smiled and nodded, handing him a glass of the guava juice that all Indians seemed to love.

"What do you do with that, *beta*?" He adjusted his round, owl-like glasses, not sure how to react to a non-medical, non-legal career route.

"She will be an ambassador, of course." My mother smiled, rubbing my back as I bent down to hand her a glass of juice. Last week, when the Sharmas had visited, I was going to work with the mayor; now she was catching on to this international thing. Once I finished passing around the snacks and drinks, my mother said, "Get your brother, *beta*."

Happy to leave the interrogation, I walked upstairs and peeked into Vijay's room. "It's time to make your grand appearance."

"Right," he said, taking one last look at his computer screen and walking out. I looked around his room, noting how tidy it was. Mama had probably cleaned it up, a perk of living at home. I wasn't jealous. I would never want her going through my things. Senior year of high school, she found a picture of me with a few friends and went berserk because I was standing with my arm around a boy. I tried explaining he was just a friend, but she had already dreamt up how I was about to be shamed in the community. Thank God for dorms at college.

I walked over to my brother's laptop and saw he had been looking at Megha's profile on the marriage website. Resourceful guy, my brother. I scrolled through her pictures to the personal info. Height: 5'1." Weight: 108. Caste: Khatri. Sub Caste: Gothar. I didn't even know what sub caste was. Blood group, occupation of siblings . . . this website had it all. I cringed at the thought of my mother making an account for me.

I lingered in my brother's room, not quite ready to go back. I guess I was as nervous as Megha. In the span of one afternoon, I could have a new sister. She was a year younger and the comparisons had already started. She had an MBA, and now she'd be married—all at a younger age than me. It wouldn't be long before Mama would start sending me bio data. I'd already heard her tell the aunties to keep an eye out for eligible bachelors. I hadn't told anyone about my final round of interviews for the Peace Corps yet. My mother would not understand wanting to live alone for two years in a foreign country. And I understood her trepidation; she had only ever lived in her parents' house and then her husband's. Just like Megha.

But that's not the life I wanted, and I was ready to put distance between myself and the life being forced on me. Maybe Megha Mehta would be the daughter I could never be.

I stopped at the downstairs bathroom to splash water on my face, to compose myself and prepare for the rest of the afternoon, the rest of my life. As I approached the door, I could smell cigarettes. No one in my family smoked. I pushed open the door and saw Megha balancing on the ledge of the bathtub, one hand holding up her *salwar* and the other on the high window ledge, holding a cigarette. That bathroom-door lock had never worked, but she didn't know that yet.

I stared at the tendrils of smoke trailing from the cigarette to the open window. "Oh, um, excuse me," I said, backing out and shutting the door. I rested my back against the closed door. I smiled. The perfect Indian daughter smoked.

Back in the living room, Mrs. Mehta was telling my mother, "I

have raised my daughter to be a great cook and housewife, Kaminiji."
I stifled a laugh—the great cook and housewife who needed her occasional nicotine fix.

Megha came back looking a bit shaken up, and I gave her what I hoped was a reassuring smile. I walked over and offered her a glass of water. It was the first time I was up close to her, and I could see her neck was about two shades darker than the face makeup she wore. Someone needed to teach this girl how to blend. As she accepted the water, her hand shook, and I looked down at her manicured nails. They were fake acrylics, and I could see remnants of the originals bitten to stubs under the French tips.

I glanced at my mother to see if she noticed any of this, but she was nodding at Mrs. Mehta, who was telling her about how Megha was making perfectly round rotis at the age of seven. My rotis still looked like the map of India.

"Yes, these girls have grown up here in America but still know our culture. My Priya makes fantastic butter chicken," my mother said. I loved my mother for bragging about me, but I actually hated butter chicken. It was too oily and spicy; it usually made me feel sick.

Vijay had been sitting silently till now. He turned to Megha, "So, what are your hobbies?"

"I like to cook, knit, and clean." Megha recited, her smile stretched too wide, revealing yellow teeth. The response was rewarded with a curt nod from her mother.

～✺～

That night when I went to bed, my mother tucked me in—the first time since I was much younger.

"I love you, *beta*." She held my face in her hands and looked deep into my eyes, like she did when I was little. I looked up into her face, noticing the wrinkles and greying hair, and felt sad to be moving so far from her, to be keeping so much a secret.

"I love you, Mama."

She smiled and turned off the light before leaving.

"Megha is how Indian girls should be. These girls from the temple walk around in short skirts, hand in hand with some boy. Don't they see how much it hurts their mothers?" my mother had said once the Mehtas left.

In the dark of my childhood room, I pulled out my phone and went to Megha's profile on Shaadi.com. "Smoking: No. Drinking: No." I knew I would tell my brother if things got serious. I imagined Megha sneaking out of her house to buy cigarettes. What would be her excuse—groceries? Ice-cream run?

I thought about my weekends, which involved dancing, shots of tequila, and nights where I didn't always make it back to my dorm room. I thought about Daniel, my Jewish ex-boyfriend my parents would never know about but who still shared my bed from time to time. My trips to Hollywood with my girlfriends to shop, done up to the nines in our short skirts and sunglasses, me always a bit afraid a relative would see and tattle to my parents.

I thought about my mother's horror if she ever found out. I imagined it would be similar to what Megha's mother would feel about the smoking. I thought about how Megha and I weren't really that much different. How we both played our part in pleasing our mothers. How we danced the same dance for years and wrapped all the distance in I love yous from far away, sealed with our greatest fears.

Someone I May Love Still

KOMAL KAPOOR

Your face is lean now,
outlines of bones
I did not know existed.
The years have hardened you,
skin silky fragile
peppered with freckles
accumulated over time.
Your eyes, once smokey grey
are now dark tunnels,
speaking of dreams
smothered to cold coal.
But when you smile,
I can still hear the laughter
bubbling out of you at six
as you licked the ice cream
running down your wrist,
gleeful and free;
when you smile, I can see
someone I may love still.

Umbilical And Invisible
Still.

Beyond the Tree Line

TYLER KNOTT GREGSON

HEY CALLED IT A DISAPPEARANCE. THEY didn't have another name for it back then, so they gave it mystery, gave it magic as if it were a trick left unfinished; someone just forgot to bring you back again. I thought of it that way for a while, if I'm honest, told myself a vanishing was better than the alternative, imagined a million scenarios that could have played out. Some helped me find sleep; others stole it, but still we didn't know and didn't know if we ever would.

I remember it fading, the missing, but I remember telling people it never did, never would. Live long enough with an ache and it starts to feel normal, stops stinging. I wouldn't have told you this, not ever. It's a guilt I think I'll take with me when I go, but these are the truths I know; this is the way I went through it. These are the letters I won't ever send, for there is nowhere to send them, no one that could deliver them to you for me. The beginning was the hardest, but all beginnings are hard. Eight months we looked for you, arm in arm in arm in arm, a whole town hunting across the fields behind the house, two dozen frozen feet in the rivers on the outside of town, everyone hoping they'd find something, the two of us hoping they wouldn't. Dad was questioned, more than all the others. Fingers were pointed, and we learned you can't unpoint a finger. It changes things, plants a divide that only knows to grow. Three times for me, three rounds of telling your story the best I knew how. Three interrogations, no bare bulbs in empty black rooms, no good cop bad cop, just questions I thought would never end. Just thirteen cups of stale coffee, just three and a half boxes of Kleenex, just the sound of my own voice becoming robotic in its exhaustion. Yes, I thought you were happy; yes, you were loved; no, we never hit you; I had no idea if you kept a diary; blue jeans and a black shirt, last I saw you; what is an enemy at eighteen? No notes, no letters, no signs of struggle in the house, no sightings of your car within a thousand miles of home. All I knew of the facts was that you were here, and then you weren't.

Start at the beginning, they said, the beginning. So, I worked my way backwards. They called it a disappearance, and I didn't know what else to call it either, but if stories of you were the magic words to bring you back, I could try.

If pressed for an admission, we would have told them we always knew you wouldn't be the valedictorian type. We never held our breath for a final speech before caps littered skies like confetti ringing in a new year. We were proud; I remember that, beaming like idiots from the bottom row of wooden bleachers, early summer sunshine raising our hands like salutes, shading our eyes just to see you across the sea of faces. We stood when you walked across the stage; I felt your father's arm wrap around my waist, and it felt like a parachute in that freefall. We both wondered, separately and only rarely spoken of together, where you would end up. What do you do when passion hasn't found its way to someone yet, you asked us. How do you know which road is the right road? School wasn't one of your things, we always knew, though somewhere along the way, we started losing track of what was. We told ourselves it was natural, the quiet that started growing between us, but I wonder now if we should've shouted across it, shaken you until words fell out, some words, any words to tie us back together. Doubt. I learned to live with it over the years. Some questions don't have answers.

You were sixteen, and I was scared to death on the front porch. Dad joked about calling all his friends to get off the roads, we laughed mostly out of courtesy, and you stood with one leg already in the car, one hand on the top of the window. Strange, which details stand out, which pieces of memory embed themselves a bit bolder than the others, which stick. I can still see the excitement in your eyes, still feel the warmth in the late autumn air; I can still feel the wish rise up in my chest like a stifled sob that I could just freeze things, right there, stop time and keep you where you were, one moment away from stepping into the rest of your life. I felt things change that day. I didn't say it out loud, but felt the distance between us stretch just a bit. I'd always imagined the cord between us intact, invisible but never actually severed, told myself I could feel you wherever you were, that I hurt when you did. I was wrong, and I knew it that day. We never got the full story from you, never pressed it, hoping the lesson learned was enough, the embarrassment and the pain combined to say all we could've said with lectures about responsibility and maturity. First time alone behind the wheel and you ended up with a fractured wrist and an overnight stay in the emergency room. I never felt a thing.

Almost a full year before the wrist, you were all oversized pants and a belt with a homemade hole cut three inches beyond the last, too much tail sticking out the loops above your left pocket. Dad tied your tie, did a decent enough job. Some men are the tie-tying type, and some men aren't. Dad always fell pretty clearly on the latter side of that fence, but fumbled his way through it. Sneakers in place of dress shoes, you told us with a half grin and one of those small laughs that leaves through your nose, you planned on dancing if you were going to a dance. Not a trace of fear. I wondered where your courage came from. I drove you, alone in the front seat while you sat silently in the back, hands folded over a plastic case holding a flower already on its way to dying. Not a single fidget from you the two miles over to your date's house (for the life of me I cannot remember her name). I couldn't stop looking in the rearview mirror, sneaking glances when I thought you were staring out the window, your hand riding on the wind that passed the car, on the space between childhood and all that comes after. I remember staying completely quiet the entire way to the high school gymnasium, offering no advice, asking you no questions, vanishing myself into the steering wheel and fading September light. Only once did I peek; only once did I adjust that mirror to hold both of you, on opposite sides of the backseat, and I saw your hand reach across that terrifying space between the two of you to rest your fingers against hers. I wondered again what seed your bravery grew from, what sunlight fed it. Homecoming, they called it, not a hint of irony in that word yet. I didn't cry until I dropped you off.

A strikeout ended your short baseball career, but you lasted the season; I'll give you that. If you got on base three times over the course of the spring, I've forgotten two of them. I remember the walk, four straight pitches into the dirt that put you on first. I cheered so loudly my throat burned and led to side-eyed looks from other parents in the stands. A ground ball and you were out at second, but I didn't care; you still slid, still tried to break up the double play, still dusted off your pants and ran back to the dugout. It's up to you, Dad said, you don't have to play again if you don't want to. And so you didn't. Folded up twice over in a bin in the crawl space, I have your jersey still, couldn't bear to let it go, so I paid the $30 replacement fee to the coach without you knowing. It still has the red dust and grass stains; it always will. Some things we can freeze.

Cooking together when you were just a shade over ten, the mess we made when Dad was out of town and you chose breakfast for dinner. If I sit quietly for a moment, I can hear the sizzle of bacon on the griddle, the microwave beeping when the berries had thawed, the music wafting in like a scent from the living room. I can see you singing into a spatula and raising your arm for me to duck under, a spin before beginning again. We ate too much, laughed too hard, and felt sick for hours afterwards, but none of that mattered. Those hours were ours, and we went to bed with a sink full of dishes and flour scattered across countertops and cabinet doors. Why is it the little seconds like these that hurt more than the big? A thousand marquee moments have come and gone, faded like ghosts, but these . . . give me a handful of these and I will feel full. I will never ask for anything more.

———

Does any of this matter, I remember asking them. How is this helping you? Some mumbling about painting a bigger picture, trying to understand who you were and why you could have vanished into thin air and ether, an exit with no puff of smoke, no mirror or curtain call. More questions into more details, and all I felt was hollow. You must have known then you'd make suspects of us both; you must have known how much it would hurt. Their questions gave way to mine. I could feel myself getting angrier, feel the bitterness swelling inside like a tumor. For every answer they demanded, I wanted two more. Why, I asked. Why you? Why us? Why now? What, I wondered, what did I do wrong; what did Dad say to you the last time he saw you? What didn't we give you? What more could we have done? How is this helping, I asked again and again. Some questions stay unanswered, they told me, repeating my own words back to me.

⸻

I think you were eight when you first learned what anger could be, what colors it could wear, the soundtrack of rage. Swimming pool, midsummer, and I still feel like it was my fault. I asked some teenage kid to stop cursing, told him there were kids swimming, told him it wasn't appropriate. Fuck you, lady, shouted across the deep end, and my mouth probably hit the concrete, footprints drying, kids warming themselves belly first on the sun-soaked ground. I don't know if you even knew what the words meant, not really, but it was enough. You rose from the water like a mythical thing and screamed before you knew which words to choose. Rage in you, and for those minutes you forgot your size, forgot the physics of things, forgot that wanting a thing to be true doesn't make it so. I tried getting to you before he did, wanting to slow you down, wanting to protect you like you were trying to protect me, but he got there first. Thirteen is old enough to blacken the eye of an eight-year-old, we learned that day, but not old enough for me to hit back. I held your chest, wet and heaving, while you cried and struggled to get back to the boy who hurt you. How were you so brave? Will you teach me what you know of ferocity?

I made birthday cakes for all your birthdays, I told them. This has no relevance, I said, but I did. Maybe if they saw that effort, they would understand how hard we always tried, how naturally it came, being there for you. Hot air balloons, whales with sharks, Volkswagen Beetles, a guitar, a castle, and a baker's dozen more, forgotten by now but for the photographs that remain. Games too, I told them, always games at the parties. We tried so hard to make it fun. I'm sure it's not your fault, they said more than once, but those words felt weightless when faced with what we were faced with. I hope I told them I appreciated the sentiment. I hope I explained away my frustration back then. I hope a lot of things, still, and wonder to myself where my own courage comes from.

Twenty-one years like a blink, twenty-one years like an eternity, and some of my hair still holds color. I refused to move, refused to give up the idea that one day, you'd need to have a home to come home to. Some days it gets so quiet in the house, only the wind through the storm door makes a sound. Dad still hasn't found his voice. Maybe it was the questions, I think to myself; maybe he answered one too many. Wordless, we still find each other in the moonlight some nights, flesh against flesh and the motions of what was romance, what was pleasure, once. You don't want to hear this I am sure, but it is part of this story, part of our story. I sing to him in the evenings, still, while he cooks dinner or I clean up after it, soft songs, and I think he enjoys them. He still holds my hand when we go on long drives, still squeezes it when something beautiful finds its way into our vision. He says he's watching the road, but I think he's always looking for you, even after all this time.

Winters are the hardest, when the cold comes and buttons up the house like a tomb. We orbit one another like moons, grazing each other from time to time but never colliding, at least not for long. Something about the darkness, the way it comes early and stays late, the way it steals sunlight from the front windows, feels too familiar. Darkness has a way of reminding you it's where we came from, where we're heading back to. Time feels too slow in the frozen months, and everything feels more like surviving than actually living. I feel you though, when steam rises on the windowpanes; I swear I can remember your tiny fingertips tracing tiny letters. Never mind this— memory is a road I try not to go down too often. Winters are the hardest, but like I said, live with an ache long enough and it starts to feel normal, starts to lose its sting. We've come through enough of them now to know we'll come through them again. Repetition is a soothing thing, if you let it be.

In the warmer months we sit on the front porch, the sounds of birdcalls in those haunted fields behind our house. We watch the light fade off behind the hills to the west, right out beyond the driveway we watched you drive away from all those years ago, wrist unbroken, not a hint of apprehension. Dad goes in before me, every night without fail. I think he is afraid of the woods out beyond the tree line. I think he hears you calling in the black like some howling thing. I think. Some questions don't have answers, I remind myself. I close my eyes and feel the warmth from the teacup in my palms, and think back to your fingertips sliding against that young girl's (whose name I still, for the life of me, cannot remember), and I think of the courage I saw in you, see in you still. I tell myself, eyes shut to the sunset glowing on the backs of my eyelids like lanterns, you left because you had to leave; you chose a life unwritten and couldn't bear a goodbye. I tell myself you were not taken, you were not harmed, you were not broken or in despair. I tell myself it was a kindness, this, that somewhere you're changing someone's world in a million better ways. I rock back and forth—for hours I do this, son—and listen to the music of the floorboards beneath me. I find a rhythm to the song and I get lost in it, long after your father has gone to sleep on moonless nights. If I do it long enough, I hear footsteps in the sounds. I hear steps, slow and shuffling, coming up the porch stairs, and I hear them grow still and steady in front of me. I tell you this because it's the only truth I know, the only one I have left to tell, and I tell it so you'll hear it somehow, for we are still connected, umbilical and invisible, still. I keep my eyes closed, for I know you are there, in front of me, and I know your face has changed. Aged and handsome, the years have worn you smooth in some places, wrinkled in others. I feel the weight of you between us, and I hear you whisper of where you've been. I pretend to open my eyes to see your eyes, tunnels now, and I wait for you to lend me that half grin. I wait and ask no questions, but when you smile, I am no longer here. I am there, years before this. I can still hear the laughter bubbling out of you as you licked the ice cream running down your wrist, I can still see the melting remains of the cone that fell, and I can still hear you tell me that it's okay, that it was good while it lasted.

I wonder, always, where your courage came from.

More Poems of
Connection and
Otherwise

When You're Other

Alicia Cook

When you're other, you will lose time.
You will be less reason, more rhyme.
You will self-medicate your mind,
to ease the havoc and clutter.
You'll sleep alone in the gutter.
Your light will crackle the sky,
you'll disrupt like thunder.
When you're other.

When your eyes see things in an obscure way,
opinions of the majority will sway,
but hardly land in your favor.

When you can make beauty out of your pain,
you'll be an outsider until you decay,
then they'll call you a trailblazer.

When you're other,
it is easy to feel alone,
though you feel you're best on your own.
It's easy to find yourself lost,
when your faith and trust have been crossed.
Easy to question your sanity,
when your art stems from tragedy.

When you're other,
the world will seem overcrowded
by perceptions that are clouded.
You will yearn for a safe haven,
a lush forest of creation.
Then, a place will call out to you,
"You are other, run for cover."

This place is
haunted and cold,
just like your soul.
Both ache to thaw
as the past claws
and wars and gnaws.

It's a place
to breathe new breath.
To gather strength.
To reach new lengths.
To shut your eyes
and count to ten.

It's a place
to dance with the skeletons in your closet,
take turns waltzing with the reasons that caused this.
As they stretch their bones and regrow their flesh,
you will thank them for creating this mess.

Because here, you will find your peace
in who you are, in how you think,
in how you see things differently.
And at the top of your lungs you will sing:

"I am other, one of a kind.
There are no flaws in my design.
You cannot keep me confined.
Stars seek me out to sleep over.
Even in dark, I find color.
I will raise up those who suffer.
I search for rain, I recover.
My light will adorn the sky,
I'll erupt like thunder.
I am other."

Dis/Reconnect

Alicia Cook

I wash six milligrams of melatonin down with iced coffee and still act surprised when I wake up in the middle of the night with a pounding heart, short of breath. I've always been this way and I used to envy the people who could just . . . be. I see words and pattern in everything, even in the phosphine light shows of my insomnia. I think in rhyme. For years my overactive brain has refused to stop, but it used to slow its pace, allow me time to catch up, to take in a sunset without thinking about what I needed to accomplish once it rose again. I'm not complaining; I have everything I have ever dreamed of having. Now if only I could sleep long enough to actually dream. And that's the disconnect.

I tell you I feel tired and you say, "But you slept for twelve hours," and I know you don't get it. I tell you maybe I need vitamin D and you crack a joke about your dick, and I know you don't get it. You tell me I have nothing to be sad about and, when I agree with you, you look at me like I have three heads, and I know you don't get it. I tell you the noise and the crowds are getting to me and you say, "If you didn't want to come, then why did you?" And I know you don't get it. I tell you my temples feel heavy and you say, "Take Advil," and I know you don't get it. You suggest maybe another shower, or makeup, or a run will lift my spirits, and I know you don't get it. And that's the disconnect.

I'm not good today. The light hurts my eyes and I left the house without washing my face, so it's 2:00 p.m. and I am still wiping away crust from the corners of my eyes. I'm not good today. The weather is affecting my mood and I am crying too easily at commercials so I put on something I've seen a trillion times. I'm not good today. I've been tired since I woke up but my mind won't quiet down enough to rest, so I light a candle at 3:18 a.m. and decide I'll call my mother later on in the morning. I'm not good today, and I'm good with that; I understand my mind and my body, and I know even though I'm down, I'm not down for the count. Rise and fall. Ebb and flow. Breathe in and out. I will not let today obstruct the potential in tomorrow. And that's the reconnect.

Castaway

RAQUEL FRANCO

We abide in this house
together
and I am more wave
than stream.
Some days are float,
gentle kiss, palm inside palm.
Some days I am all rage,
siren voice that nothing can calm.
Other days I am drowning,
taking these walls down with us.
Depression turned
this once-girl
into an ocean-woman
and I love you for surviving,
setting sail
knowing
you might never see land.

Look in the Mirror

Raquel Franco

I tell her she is too fat.
Waist too thick, cheeks too round.
Shove a pizza down her throat
to make her forget
but she does not forget.
She misses the jut of hip bone
that she used to squeeze
between her fingers
to remind her
she was a body worthy of being loved.
Today touching her own skin
is a mere memory.
Her hands strangers to
her own belly.
I tell her I do not love her.
All loose skin and lazy tendons,
thick hips and stubby legs.
This extra weight she carries
is just evidence of her circumstance,
the result of a woman
who cannot control herself,
a woman who used to work out,
who wants to work out
but still chooses the couch.
I tell her
I find her disgusting
but I know
she is not disgusting.
One day I will love her
no matter what.

Komal Kapoor

We were running in a field of purple
beside the crumbling Great Wall
and came upon water,
road suddenly turned to cliff.
"Look, the ocean," I cried.
"What's that?" you said.
"You live here; how do you not know?
This, this water, the ocean!"
"Oh, I did not know it had a name," you said,
looking up at where the ocean was in the sky
with polar bears and penguins afloat,
waving down with glee.
"Where are we?" I yelled,
over the waves of ocean green
like the inside of a Philip Pullman scene.
"This is my home,
I wanted you to see," you said
and I felt your hand in mine,
as though it had been there all my life.
And we ran and ran,
wild and free in a magical land
we ran and ran
together, hand in hand.

KOMAL KAPOOR

Our promises envelop us,
cocooning us in a gentle mist of love
lifting us higher and higher.
I had forgotten what it is like
to indulge in emotion
but you, my dear, have the rare gift
of making me f e e l.

TYLER KNOTT GREGSON

I didn't know the bed was so big
Until you filled the space between us
With a continent of silence.
You the City of Angels
And I the city that never sleeps,
Opposite coast, still awake
And waiting.

Please say something, make your
Words your wagon and send it
Across the grasslands to retrieve me.
I will be the pioneer you need,
The gold rush believer
Searching out the shine in you.
Just speak.

How boring a word, beautiful, how overused, how trite, cliche. There's gotta be another way to tell you what I see, to explain. Does it tell you that you slow time, for me, does it explain the way I've seen traffic patterns change, because you found your way across a street? It's not a full enough word, beautiful, to demonstrate how your heart lives mostly out of your chest, beating for those you love, forgetting to circle it back onto yourself. This is a beautiful thing. That word again, that boring, incomplete word.

Maybe I'll invent a way to invent new words, a machine that crams in many and spits out one, one perfect word for each way you're astounding into me. Two quarters, maybe three, a metal slide and that nostalgic shlunk sound when they go in and turn it on. What will it say, what fortune will it spit out, what new entry into an unpublished dictionary will I receive when I say

AcheLookingAtYouIFeelTheWeightOfEveryRegretLiftEvery-FearScreamItsFinalScreamAndRefuseToWonderWhatLife-WouldBeWithoutYouBesideMeAndDon'tUnderstandHowY ouCanMakeEveryoneFeelLikeABetterVersionOfTheThemThey-ManageToPresentToThisMixedUpWorldAndSecretlyHopeY-ouNeverFigureOutThatIProbablyDon'tDeserveYouButIW illKeepTryingToEarnItInTheOffChanceYouDoOneDayLearnThisI-AcheLookingAtYouIAcheIAcheIAche

We'll see, I guess, but it better not be beautiful. It's too damn boring.

Spook Light Road

NOAH MILLIGAN

In Ottawa County Oklahoma
tucked by the Missouri border,
my father, mother, brother, and I
once visited Spook Light Road.

This was a year before
my brother's DUI
and nineteen before
my own.

To prove I was not afraid
I joined my brother
up the dirt road to watch
the Spook Light on the horizon.

To this day, my mother swears
a man stood with my brother and me
although we could not see him,
telling us things we could not hear.

This was eight years before
his overdose
and eight and a day before
Mom found his body.

I still don't believe
she saw the man there,
although I sometimes wonder
what harm it would cause
if I told her I did.

Spook Light Road is now paved over,
and I too am hardened,
more like the Spook Light:
a burning ball
of incandescent rage

Down Western

Noah Milligan

I once took an Uber to have drinks with my friends,
and the driver told me a body had been buried in her yard.
It had been there at least a year, interred by the woodshed
until all that remained was bone blackened by wet earth.
She said this nonchalantly, as if asking which direction
Broadway Extension or down Western
because down Western the traffic may be bad
but the view was just that much better.
I asked her what she did once she'd found the body,
and she said she'd buried it deeper, of course,
because she was a woman who rushed to tie her shoes
when her laces have come undone.

COURTNEY PEPPERNELL

The universe stretched out before me
in a thousand galaxies of dreams
living side by side in close proximity
  yet rarely is anything as it seems

Somehow love letters turned into smartphones
and months at sea turned into boarding planes
  and meeting in new countries

But there are days I feel such longing
a solitude I cannot seem to escape
and even if the distance between us
has become so fragile and small
the days still move so slowly
  how did I end up so lonely

We were tangled in sheets, coffee cups by the bed. I'd been watching you as you slept, because for years I've never been able to get you out of my head. They said we couldn't get married, they tried to enforce this space between us, told us we were sinners and that the love we shared wasn't real. They were trapped in their own hate, separated from the world moving forward, disconnected from all the things these new beliefs awarded. But we held on, fused our hearts together, and in the end the fear and judgement could not divide us. Because I'll love you in every lifetime, I'll protect you every day, I'll fight for the love we share, no matter what they say.

Swimming in Circles on Plenty of Fish

K. Y. ROBINSON

there is an app for everything. a new way to use your hands for what the mouth cannot say.
an ocean of possibilities. salt in the air for the taking. where love floats for sirens & flounders for sea monsters. there are 159 men online within a 10-mile radius. will any of them find me attractive? i'm in a losing battle against my biological clock. as i ripen with age, gravity becomes stronger & drags at my youth. my body carries too much in the middle. too much chicken. oxtails. candied yams. collard greens. for the culture. for the trauma. for the heart that is always breaking.

will my sense of humor, love for the arts & kindness be enough in this day & age? my heart cracks open with hope but not too much. i wait for right swipes & matches. i watch ellipses rise & fall like tides. i swipe & scroll until my fingertips feel like they've been stung by bees. i receive more degrading messages than soft ones. when the loneliness becomes a wildfire, i read them just to feel the words burn. the loneliness contemplates being the good gargantuan girl they expect. to gratefully devour their godheads whole. to be their secret shame in the shadows.

is some attention better than none if i become ashes in the end? i gather slivers of my self-esteem & tell myself: *i'm tired of swimming in circles. i want to find love. to be the catch of a lifetime. to be a siren song—not an interlude.*

Always Been America

K. Y. Robinson

you say this isn't
the america you know as if:
the amber waves of grain
wither in your hands.
purple mountain majesties
melt into the sea.
fruited plains leave
a bitter taste in your mouth.
the thorny crown of brotherhood
snuffs out the dawn's early light.

o say why you can't see
the unholy remnants of
strange fruits hanging
from southern trees.
the weary who chant
& march to overcome it all.
bullets that bury themselves
in black rib cages
& end their bloom.

justice is elusive
as a fistful of sand.
find me a hallelujah
that isn't on cinderblocks.
a prayer that don't sound
like a broken record.

this is the america I know—
an unhinging jaw.
a mouth foaming with hate.
it just has more permission
to show its teeth now.
you only see the storm
when it heads your way.

What You Didn't Know

CAITLYN SIEHL

Oh, to be ravaged by loneliness
by its soft, malleable teeth.
A slow death.
A slow ravaging.
More like being swallowed than eaten.

You used to beg God for this
at night,
used to beg him to make
you small enough to get picked up in something's
mouth and carried away like a seed.

What you didn't know
was that nothing that wanted
you had claws.

The Cup of Love

CAITLYN SIEHL

You drink from the cup
of love until you runneth over,
Pink blood filling in the tile
like it will keep the house together.

Do you remember the first flush of heat?
The first time you pressed
your mouth against something that could bite
but didn't?

How it felt to want to die
but not being able to stomach it?
If they'd let you go hungry
you would've chewed your
own heart out,
clamped down on it so hard
the wind could tunnel through
the teeth marks.

You eat from the bowl of life
until your belly swells.
You eat until you runneth over,
until you runneth over,
until your mouth spills
into the cool porcelain,
until all your teeth fall out
and you're just tongue.

Do you remember starving?
Do you remember the sound of blood
in your ears?
How it felt to bite down
and taste nothing?
Finally nothing?

No one in the world
could handle your hunger, girl.
No one in the world could survive it.

Excerpt from the Diaries of a Winged Creature

N. L. Shompole

1

Lover, I hope you understand that I lived for the moments you made me laugh. I lived for the sound of your heartbeat the hour when the sky was still more dark than light. Lover, I hope you understand that sometimes I missed you until my sternum ached, but I never saw your face in my dreams.

> I hope you understand that I only ever dreamed of growing feathers. I hope you understand that I looked for you in my dreams, but they were only ever about the sky, my dreams were only about the sky.

Lover, I hope you understand that I was never easy to know, that my eyes were always too dark for divining, and the psychic around the corner wasn't lying when she warned you of how I would break your heart.

> I hope you understand now that it broke me to see all that grief on your face. I hope you know that I never meant to break your heart. I hope you know your pain haunts me still.

2

Lover, I hope you will remember when I told you the sky had my heart. Lover, I hope you know how much I miss your fingers on my skin, a slow burning, a devouring. Lover, I hope you know that in your arms I was everything.

> I hope you understand that I missed you, but not enough to tether me to the ground, never enough to keep me from the sky.

Lover, I hope you understand that I only ever dreamed of growing wings, I only ever dreamed of the sharp wind against my skin. Lover, I hope you understand that I wanted to stay but I have only ever dreamed of taking flight.

> I hope you understand that you were enough, but that no one, not even you, could replace the sky.

Those Who Went

N. L. SHOMPOLE

In November a crow-feathered boy cannibalizes himself,
body found ravaged, still hungering for light.

He took flight on the cusp of the cold season, outbound on the
tailwind of a thousand dreams woven like destination, like map, like
veins on the inside of elbow, purpling with life.

Frost season the crow-skinned boy tailspins, reeling back-
wards out of mauve-bodied sea, pulled out of sky-orbit by
radio static.

He calls home three minutes after midnight, frantic. Each hello
echoes and caws and caws through phone lines voice stretched along
black wire because sound needs tether to span the ocean.

Sometimes the neighbor watches him through window
blinds, reverse migrant caught in the wrong hemisphere
out of season.

He never answers when she asks him what he's doing, spinning
round and round and round in the parking lot, black eyes bolted to
the sky. Searching, always searching for the way home.

Water season the crow-eyed boy hails this new arrival.
Sky vacillates between dark and darker. Night so long he
names the stars after faces he only ever sees in dreams
now.

Lately the neighbor has taken to leaving food on his doorstep. Roast pigeon and casserole and plum pie the color of sparrow blood in June. He feasts and thirsts by turns, hunger beast-like, a dark devouring caught too deep in lockstep with disaster.

> Sun season the crow-boned boy is more frail than a whisper.

He sleeps and wakes in fits, ossified heart beats in tandem with the tide. Far-gone lungs black like coal, obsidian body brittle with anguish.

> Harvest season the crow-hearted boy finds himself wingless. Lost, a stranger in a country with two faces, neither of them facing the sun.

At twilight a crow-toothed boy caught in retrograde plummets towards horizon.

WILDER

my eyes are letting go like spring
and i'm losing sight of the flowers
that are asking for my rain,
because these streets are full of a city
that never sleeps and glass giants
reaching upward to a sky where the
trees once lived.

the light is blinding—
blinking at a night that
already knows how to shine
and i can't help but wonder
if the plane in the distance
can see through the haze.

and when you look in my direction,
i hope you notice the way
i carry the wild with my hands.
i'm growing towards the light, and
you're still opening your eyes.

WILDER

today i held a butterfly.
it was beautiful like the
stained-glass view you loved
from our corner of the world.
and as it flew away before
i could kiss it goodbye, i waved,
knowing i couldn't hold something
that wanted me to let it go.

Contributors

Alicia Cook is a writer and activist living in New Jersey whose words have been highlighted in *Teen Vogue, CNN,* and *USA Today*. She is the author of *Stuff I've Been Feeling Lately* and *I Hope My Voice Doesn't Skip*. She is dedicated to shedding light on how drug addiction impacts entire families.

Twitter: @the_alicia_cook
Instagram: @thealiciacook

Raquel Franco is a wife, mother, friend, sister, daughter, and poet. Her work has been featured on *Thought Catalog* and *Harness Magazine*. She is the author of the poetry collection, *Keep Me Wild*, and is featured in the poetry compilation *Crown Anthology*.

Twitter: @wordsbyraquel
Instagram: @raquelfranco.poet

Tyler Knott Gregson is a poet, photographer, artist, and author of *Chasers of the Light, All the Words Are Yours, Wildly into the Dark, North Pole Ninjas,* and *Miracle in the Mundane.* When he's not writing, he operates Chasers of the Light Photography, and photographs weddings and travel all over the globe with his fiancée, Sarah Linden.

@tylerknott

Komal Kapoor is a Los Angeles based writer originally from the Punjab, India. She's passionate about helping individuals express themselves and identify their strengths, most recently shared through her TEDx talk. She is the author of *Unfollowing You*.

@komalesque

Noah Milligan is an author living in Norman, OK whose short fiction has been published in dozens of literary journals. He is the author of *An Elegant Theory*, which was a finalist for Foreword Indies Book of the Year and the Horatio Nelson Fiction Prize; the short story collection *Five Hundred Poor*; and the novel *Into Captivity They Will Go*.

@MilliganNoah

Courtney Peppernell is the best-selling author of *Pillow Thoughts*. Courtney has traveled extensively through Europe, England, USA, Indonesia, New Zealand. She lives in Sydney, Australia with her partner, Rhian, and their dogs, Hero and Dakota.

Twitter: @courtpeppernell
Instagram: @courtneypeppernell

K. Y. Robinson is an introverted writer based in Houston, Texas. She received a BA in journalism and MA in history from Texas Southern University. She has loved words pressed against pages since childhood, and has been chasing them ever since. She is the author of *The Chaos of Longing* and *Submerge*.

@iamkyrobinson

N. L. Shompole is a Kenyan-born multi-platform artist. Her written and photographic works have been featured in various publications. She is also the author of several poetry collections including the best-selling collection *Lace Bone Beast: Poems & Other Fairytales for Wicked Girls*.

Twitter: @luciasolaris
Instagram: @nlshompole

Caitlyn Siehl is a poet and big sad baby from New Jersey. She is the author of the poetry collections *What We Buried* and *Crybaby* and traveled the country in her little Honda Civic while crying over a Dungeons and Dragons podcast.

@caitlynsiehl

Wilder is an old soul, writer, creator, designer, artist, explorer, and lover of the wild. From an open window in Chicago, she collects everyday moments and brings them to life through words and imagery. Her creative journey began as a child when she used to paint the sky on the back of her hands so the folded paper cranes resting on the bedroom floor had a reason to fly.

@wilderpoetry

Michelle Halket is a bibliophile and technophile who loves to try new things, which is what prompted her to start a digital-first publishing company when very few people knew what ebooks were. When she's not fully immersed in words, devices, and paper stock, she spends time with her family and dog in the forests of Vancouver.

@centavepub

Notes

Poets to Watch

The morning sky seemed to melt into itself. The clouds cleared and bowed as the sun peeked over the horizon. Yellows and purples blended together creating lilac poetry within the sunrise. As I drove farther from your house, as I put more miles between us, I looked up and saw what God had painted for me.

That's when I knew that everything was going to be okay. Definitely not today, probably not tomorrow, maybe not for a long while . . .

but eventually.

MAKENZIE CAMPBELL grew up in the Pacific Northwest and has been expressing herself through poetry since grade school. Makenzie is pursuing a degree in psychology at Washington State University, and her little free time is spent traveling and exploring the wild trails of the Cascades.

She is the author of the best-selling book *2am Thoughts*.

@makenzie.campbell.poetry

Photographs

I'm a tween, and my mother and I are
shopping at the grocery store, and for some hazy reason
I don't remember, I see she's got that photo in her purse,
the one I hate.
The one where her ribs curve
inward so sharply
to her concave belly it actually hurts me to see it,
where her hair is shorn russet red and her eyes so big
in her skull she is nearly dead.
I say, Why would you carry that around?
I don't recall her answer. I do remember thinking it was a trophy,
do remember cans of soup on the store shelves,
do remember thinking of other photos of my mother:

A chubby, cherubic toddler with dimples in her cheeks,
white dress, ruffled socks, blond curls,
standing, lone on a prairie;

A 1960s Polaroid, my mother posed
on a bed, mint-green peignoir
and soft high-roller curls in carrot-red;

On her and my father's honeymoon (he has always, always said she is
beautiful),
sitting on a dock in cut-off jean shorts and white tank,
strong shoulders, head thrown back,
laughing.

God, my mother has a beautiful smile.
I think she looks like Maureen O'Hara; I think she looks like my sister.
I think she looks nothing like me.
And I wonder why, when you are so very great,
would you try to make yourself so damn small?

Later, I'll get it. I will hear all the ways in which we try to lose ourselves
in this world, and I will deduce for myself all the ways in which I am
wrong.
Then I'll crave the same emptiness inside me.
I will gobble it up like I am starving for air instead of
food: hungry, on my knees forcing my finger
down my throat, exercising in my room at night, failing
gym because I think I'm too fat to get in the pool,
up and down and on the scale, embarrassed of this flesh,
these marks on my skin, this number on my tag.
Even now when I am thirty-six, I am still trying to fall back in love
with my body, still healing from all the ways in which I have hurt it,
still trying to forgive this cruel world
for making so many of us feel so much less than.

But at that moment, standing in the middle of the store,
staring at my mother's starving face captured by a camera,
I think,
I will never understand why,
with so many photographs,
this is the one she chooses to carry.

AMANDA LINSMEIER is the author of two poetry books, *Like Waves* and *Our Wild
Magic*. She lives in a small house in the woods where she's busy writing dark
fairytales, raising little beasties, and drinking plenty of iced coffee.

@amandalinsmeier

Safe

you say, almost under your breath, as the car stops outside my home
Safe, you say again
and it is indeed the state in which I am dispatched at Chelsea Street,
I get out of your car, filled with music,
thank you and touch your shoulder
but your dark eyes are fixed on the road ahead.

Earlier,
when I rolled the soft consonants of your name towards you,
you returned my own name so gently, it felt like a caress.

Then, shortly before we left,
you walked closer and put your hand on my back,
I really liked the weight of it, but for some reason I stiffened
and you retreated—
an unwinding coil rewound.

Somewhere in-between:
friends and strangers mill around us, on their way to pool tables,
chequered
dance floors, graffiti-walled bathrooms or dark corners of their own.
And for a long short while
we sit on top of a table in the dark
side by side
while I smoke your cigarettes and you listen to my 3am thoughts
and you make me laugh and I try to pry your stories loose
as my legs dangle in time to the husky song
of your voice at my ear.

CARLA KREUSER is a designer, illustrator, and occasional poet, with a penchant
for horror stories and binding her own illustrated books by hand.

@skallakind

Athena

you say I'm like a god to you,
and I almost play along

god of kitchen appliances
mouth like a tea kettle who
needs to be heard

god of all things delicate
fingers that will wring you out
harder than the washer and lips
that speak poetry more than kindness

god of striking matches and lighting
myself on fire for the show

god of breaking myself just
so people don't get bored

JADE HOMA is a poet and inter-sectional feminist who prides herself on
being soft. She is the editor of *Storm of Blue.*

@jadehoma

At Sea

The roads are empty.
The wind
Runs its hands
through my hair.
Fluorescent orange beams
pave my path.
They are my only light,
as the moon is new.

My heart is held together
with strips of tape.
Each strip
represents the love
I have been fed
since the time of break.
Some stay stuck,
refusing to peel.
Others are losing their grip,
as tears dampen their efforts.

The divide is heavy.
Each side having its
own thoughts
and desires.
I so desperately
want to return home,
to familiar faces
and the warmth
of my bedsheets.
To wake every morning
knowing that I wasn't alone.

But I was.
I felt so alone,
like a man at sea.

F. S. YOUSAF is a poet from New Jersey. He is the author of *Sincerely*.

@fsyousaf

In Remembering

lightning flashes
just beyond a
ripe and swaying field
thick as honey
because of its distance
it is an empty mouth

I consider what has once been whispered
a name, a date, an expiration

I recall my mother's wheat-gold hair
bending—just before twilight—
in a mid-summer breeze
few things are as sweet
as moments of rebirth
air so heavy with moisture
I collect it in my palms and drink

another flicker against the
darkening underbelly of clouds
followed closely by the shadow
of a tremble, then

quiet

WILLIAM BORTZ is a husband, poet, and editor from Iowa.

@willbortz

WANT MORE? CHECK OUT [DIS]CONNECTED VOLUME 1

[DIS]CONNECTED

POEMS & STORIES OF CONNECTION AND OTHERWISE

SARA BOND

NIKITA GILL

PIERRE ALEX JEANTY

AMANDA LOVELACE

CANISIA LUBRIN

TRISTA MATEER

CYRUS PARKER

YENA SHARMA PURMASIR

LIAM RYAN

R. H. SWANEY

IAIN S. THOMAS

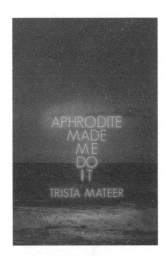

Alicia Cook

Raquel

caitlyn siehl